The Flower Collection

DANIELLE TEMPESTA

Quote

What a beautiful world where vanilla is a flower
and chocolate is a tree.

Dedication

*To the museum fuddy duddies for memories
that will last a lifetime.
This may be a romance novel, but this book is my love letter
to the museum that changed my life.*

⚓ Part One ⚓

Violet

Chapter 1

She stared at the bones before her. Unlike freshly exposed bones that are white and gleaming, these were dark brown, fossilized, and massive above her. The bones she marveled at were one of the greatest scientific discoveries in modern days. Paleontologists, fossil preparators, and exhibition handlers were all standing by as the world's largest and most complete *Tyranosaurus rex* was being dismantled from its home in the main hall of the museum. Also standing under the slow, deliberate disassembly of the fossil specimen was the museum's Collection Assistant of Botany, Veronica Sterling.

Although Veronica was simply on her way into work, she knew the strategic move of the museum's beloved *T. rex* was taking place that day. She loved everything about the natural history museum and had to stop to admire the rest of the museum staff at work.

The skull of the specimen was being removed next, and Veronica stared with bated breath and watched the staff carefully, slowly, remove the skull from the rest of the mounted fossil.

Media was present to document this moment at the museum, as well as the museum's staff photographer. The museum received funding to dedicate an entire exhibition hall to this famed specimen, and today was the day the process began. Press photographers and journalists had cameras out, watching the labor through their photo lenses all around Veronica. She had her cell phone in hand, filming the moment too.

When the skull broke free from the mounted frame, the rest of the specimen shook from the force. An exhibitions team member was on a ladder near the torso of the fossil, and grabbed the tiny arm of the specimen to keep it steady.

Veronica inadvertently gasped as she watched the massive fossil shake, and looked around her, as if to say, *did you just see that?* Everyone else felt the tension in the air, too. Veronica's eyes darted from person to person sheepishly, feeling slightly embarrassed that she gasped out loud. Her eyes stopped on a face she had never seen before, a tall man standing off on his own, with a backpack, as if he too had just walked in the door. Resting casually on top of his head was a thick, blue beanie, almost hiding his hair, except for the ends which were waves around his neck.

He was handsomely tan, with dark hair and an attractive face. He must have felt Veronica's gaze on him, because he looked over and they locked eyes.

Feeling caught, Veronica looked away, seeking a familiar face. She caught the eyes of Frances, a colleague she knew well that worked in the public relations department, and they shot each other a look, as if to say, "Another day at work!"

Veronica smiled at her coworker and decided to make her way to the Division of Botany. Days like this were what she loved most about working at the museum. She had her own work that she was proud of in botany, but most of all, she was inspired by the mission of the museum, and making science and natural history accessible to all.

She collected flowers for as long as she could remember. She pressed them between books, magazines, and stacks of mail. Eventually, she would transfer them to individual papers, each one gently taped down, with notes on where the flower came from.

Her parents lived the suburban life with a house and a front yard and a garden in the back that her mother attended to nearly every weekend. They spent a lot of time outdoors, which would explain where her love for plants came from, and how she came to study botany.

Her mother nurtured the garden, researching ways to ensure the gardenias had the most blooms the following season. She enjoyed taking clippings from her garden to put in vases around the house. Her oldest daughter, Veronica, on the other hand, was the type to feel like a cut flower is only enjoyed in the moment, while a flower blooming on the plant can be enjoyed by all for longer.

The collecting started as a way to make the cut flowers last longer. To only have them in a vase for a few days felt wasteful to her. For her mom, she felt she enjoyed them more when they were perched on the kitchen table or next to the sink for her to see each morning when having her coffee. Her daughter began pressing them in between the pages of books to make the clippings worth it. This way, they would last forever.

Her mom loved gardening, so it would make sense that she would name her daughter Veronica, after a flower. It almost felt like it was written from the start that Veronica would appreciate nature, particularly plants.

These days, Veronica still has her modest, private collection of pressed flowers and plants. She moved them from her parents' home, and then from one student housing apartment to another. Now, she lives in an apartment in the city, on the second floor of a two-flat with the smallest square of a front yard. The patch of grass along the fence is just big enough for the downstairs neighbor's dog to use to relieve himself quickly in the winter when it's too cold for a proper walk. Not quite large enough for a garden. In summer, there are chairs set out under the short tree in the front yard, which is a tranquil spot for people-watching as they come and go from the dive bar across the street.

Spring was approaching, so Veronica was still taking the train to work, the last of the cold days just barely behind her. In summer, she preferred to ride her bike to the museum, bypassing the crowds and avoiding the waiting time, biking along the lake that the museum sat on. The earth was welcoming spring with small buds of tulips in the gardens around the city, and in the gardens of the museum campus.

The museum building itself was neoclassical style, the exterior boasting huge columns made of gray stone. Inside, the floor was limestone, and if one looked close enough, they could see fossils in the giant tiles that kept the museum fossils company at night. The museum had its own smell, somewhat musty and chemical, to keep the collections from deteriorating at an accelerated rate, yet familiar and comforting all the same.

After watching the *T. rex* dismantle, Veronica headed to her office on one of the staff-only floors of the museum. It was small, but cozy, enough space for a few desks and chairs, collection cabinets for specimens she was currently working on, and a narrow window that let in a little daylight with its unassuming view of the downtown skyline beyond the museum.

She placed her coat and her bag on the corner of her desk, figuring she would get more settled later. She quickly looked down at her outfit, assessing if she needed to primp. Veronica's wardrobe consisted mostly of thrift store specials, in which she often paired a vintage find with something more contemporary. She was inspired by the classic look of librarians and teachers, finding that all her years in academia stayed with her to this day.

Her office desk was practically covered, piles of papers, binders, and specimen packets threatening to topple over if one more item was added. While it looked a little chaotic to anyone else, Veronica knew exactly where to find anything she needed. Everything within arm's reach was categorized in her own organization system that made sense to her.

Thinking twice about keeping it on or taking it off, Veronica unraveled her scarf from her neck endlessly, cascading her dark waves of hair messily across her shoulders. The length of her hair hit just below her collarbones and framed her face. Her nose was one of her most memorable features, turning up at the end in a way that her little sister teased her about endlessly, calling her an elf or fairy. Veronica's signature nose was only ever outshone when she smiled and her pointy canines gleamed in a way that would rival a vampire's.

Veronica finger-combed her hair blindly as she walked out of her office. She had a meeting with her boss that she had to get to, she didn't have time to smooth her hair.

Veronica headed to her boss' office, only to not find him there. She knew him well enough to know that he would be in the botany collections if he wasn't at his desk. She made the walk down the staff hallway to the collections area. The walls held artifacts, objects, and specimens from the museum collections that were once on display but were rotated out for more contemporary exhibitions.

She tapped her badge to the card reader, and it blinked, unlocking the door to let her into the herbarium. Before her were rows and rows of cabinets, each one filled with folders of vascular plant specimens, pressed on large pieces of cardstock paper. Some cabinets were filled with plant-based medicines in jars, and textiles and artifacts made from plants. Others were filled with folded paper packets of messier plants like mosses and lichens.

Around the perimeter of the room were counters that housed specimens that were being actively studied or inventoried, computers as ancient as the specimens in the collection, maps pinned up on display, and scientific journals on the shelves that spanned the entire length of the wall. The museum collections areas felt lived in; binders were stacked precariously on top of each other, threatening to topple if someone dared to stack another on top. Clear glass cabinet doors protected dusty brown book covers holding the old catalog systems of the collections.

"William?" she called out, making her way to the far wall, looking down each aisle of cabinets to spot him.

"Back here," his voice called, from the general direction of cabinets filled with moss. Veronica stopped at the aisle with a label that simply said, "Bryophyta."

"Are we still meeting?" she asked when she spotted him. William had been the Collections Manager of Botany at the museum for decades. He was now in his fifties, what was left of his hair was graying, but his enthusiasm and passion for his work at the museum was full of life. He brought Veronica on as the Collections Assistant of Botany shortly after she received her Master's Degree. His specialty was moss and lichens, and her graduate studies on neotropical botany was the perfect complement to the museum's collection.

"Yes, let's meet. I'm working on my symposium now, and needed to reference some bryophyte specimens, but I've reached a stopping point," he replied, holding a paper specimen packet filled with moss. William placed the glasses that hung from his neck on the tip of his nose to study the packet.

"Ah, referencing the old murder moss, are you?" Veronica teased.

William laughed as he approached her. "It's the most memorable botany specimen we have. I don't miss a chance to bring it up, especially at a scientific conference."

She followed him to a workstation where he had a computer booted up. His symposia abstract illuminated the screen along with a list of tasks he needed to complete prior to the conference.

Also on the screen was the latest museum e-newsletter, the paragraph above the fold featuring a large donation that was recently given to the museum, specifically for the anthropology collection.

"Anthropology always gets funding," Veronica sighed, taking a seat in a mismatched chair next to William's.

William looked at Veronica, then to the computer screen, registering that she must have read the newsletter that was up on his screen.

"Ah, yes. Their artifacts are impressive, easy to think of them as irreplaceable. People find them memorable, and when it comes to a wealthy family making a donation in order to be remembered, it's no surprise that they should choose a legacy that is big, flashy, bold, like the anthropology collections," William said, matter of fact.

"Yes, yes and the botany specimens are small, faded, and old," she quipped back, making William laugh. "The only time botany was publicized was when you identified a moss specimen that helped solve a murder."

"Listen, I'm very proud of that moment. It was the one time I felt like a rock star in the scientific community," he defended proudly.

"As you should be! What I'm trying to understand is how that department gets funding to have entire exhibition halls revamped and for a visiting scientist fellowship, meanwhile the plant exhibition hall has been the same since the museum opened, and the botany division relies solely on volunteers," she felt deflated.

"More funding for any of the divisions and collections is definitely something I've championed for the museum in general.

But there's only so much funding to go around, only a finite number of donors. Even with only 1% of the museum collections on display in exhibition halls, donors tend to want to fund projects that are public-facing, artifacts on display, with their names right next to them," William explained, with sympathy. "Are you still able to get your work done with the volunteers, or are you at capacity?"

"We get the work done," Veronica assured him. It was true, the volunteers she oversaw were passionate enough to do the work for experience they could put on their resume and a better chance at a job at the end of it, while also gaining potential to be incredible scientists. "We digitized more of the collection in the last year than any previous year. We've built a great process -"

"*You*'ve built a great process," William interrupted, ensuring she knew that the success of the digitization program was due to her.

"Yes, and I'd love to get funding to upgrade our equipment to capture higher quality scans of the specimens. To get computers that are younger than me." William gave her a look, and she added, "I know, I know - they're not that old. Then we would really have a problem."

"Let's talk about the conference. I was invited to speak at a symposium at the Association of Natural History Collections Forum," William said.

"Yes, which is awesome. What can I help with? Preparing some slides? Referencing some digitized specimens for the presentation?"

"Actually, I'm all set with my presentation, I still have some time to refine it," he said, pausing to gauge her reaction as he added, "I actually wanted to run an idea by you. One of the presenters of a 10-minute talk at the conference can't travel last minute. Instead of scrapping the presentation, the conference organizers are hoping to fill the spot."

Veronica felt like one of the old computers in front of them, her brain's hard drive buzzing loudly as it loaded and processed the information she was just given.

"Are you suggesting me?" she asked in disbelief.

"I think it's the natural next step in your career," he encouraged.

She thought about it for a moment, her mind spinning and thinking through the process of submitting an abstract, and what it would mean if she actually got accepted. "What would I even submit as a topic for my abstract?"

"What we just talked about - the digitization process you built, of course."

Veronica considered it. It was a project she was really proud of, having started at the museum two years ago, when the idea for digitizing the collections for scientists to access all over the globe was just that – only an idea. She took the bare bones of a plan and ran with it, sourcing dedicated volunteers that helped her turn the idea into reality.

Surely, if she could do that, she could present for 10-minutes about it to a group of fellow scientists, right?

"Alright, I'll do it. When is the deadline to submit?" she asked, mapping out the tasks ahead.

William beamed, "The sooner the better, I'll send you the link with all of the specifications on title, abstract, author information, everything you'll need to gather for submitting. Take a look, and if you have any questions, let me know."

⚓

Veronica returned to her office and before she even turned on her work computer, she took out her phone and texted her best friend.

VERONICA: *SOS, I need your help*

CAMILLA: *Did you finally order a gua sha?*

Veronica scoffed. Camilla had been trying to convince her that Korean beauty products would change her life.

VERONICA: *No, but I agreed to submit a presentation to a conference for natural history collections. And I need your editing skills.*

CAMILLA: *Who are you and what have you done with Veronica?*

CAMILLA: *In all seriousness, I'm free this week. Let's order a pizza and chat through it?*

VERONICA: *THANK YOU!*

Veronica's shoulders softened and lowered from her ears as she breathed deep. She felt overwhelmed with the added workload of having to submit a presentation, and then the impending work of actually giving a talk. It was almost enough for her to call it quits before she even submitted.

If she had known then that the conference would bring her more than just career advancement, she might have set aside her feelings of overwhelm to see everything change.

Chapter 2

Later in the week, Veronica rushed home from work to meet with her friend.

Expectedly, the doorbell rang and Veronica rushed downstairs to open the door. The first thing she saw was a pizza box. Holding it was her dearest friend, Camilla.

"Let's eat!" Camilla exclaimed, her shaggy black hair a blur as she rushed past Veronica up the stairs to her apartment. She closed the door and followed behind her friend, the scent of oven fresh pizza trailing in her wake.

Once inside the apartment, Camilla elegantly kicked off her boots without dropping the pizza box. She had her own sense of style, never conforming to trends, and instead she was the type to start trends.

Kind of like Veronica's apartment, Camilla's clothes never matched. Patterns clashed with patterns, colors competing for attention. And yet, her outfits always worked.

Like Camilla's wardrobe, Veronica's furniture in her apartment came from various thrift stores and antique shops throughout the years. Veronica forced different styles together overtime, but it worked when placed all together in her own mismatched way. A worn and well-loved couch was the centerpiece atop a vintage rug, and piles of patterned pillows were stuffed against the back of the couch, and thick, woven blankets cascaded onto the floor.

Veronica's living room walls were painted a light green, which was not very vibrant compared to all the lush plants that she had in pots around the room, some even sitting in the deep windowsills to soak up the coveted Midwest sun. The artwork on the walls were also treasures found in various thrift shops. Veronica breathed new life into them by giving them a second chance, a second home.

Camilla worked as a content marketer for an agency downtown. She was the ultimate hype woman, always there to support her friends, and constantly boosting people's self-esteem. While biology and museums were not her specialty, writing and marketing were. Camilla was unapologetically honest, so Veronica could count on her honest feedback on how to best improve her chances of getting accepted into the conference program.

Veronica had already written her conference presentation application, ready for her dearest friend to review it. She needed Camilla to help refine the title of the presentation to be catchy, but also informative. In addition, the abstract was limited to 250 words, so it needed to describe the presentation thoroughly, but at the same time, it needed to sell Veronica as a speaker.

"Start from the beginning, how did this come about?" Camilla asked.

"My boss is presenting as part of a symposium for the conference. And while he was actually invited by the conference organizers to speak, he said the next logical step for me in my career would be to submit an abstract to present in one of the scientific sessions."

"Got it. Where do we start?"

"Thank you so much for agreeing to do this. I don't have an academic advisor anymore like I did during undergrad, so William has agreed to review it before I submit it to the conference. However, I really wanted another pair of eyes on my submission before it even gets to him. So again, thank you," Veronica reiterated to her how grateful she was for her support.

"What else are friends for?" Camilla sighed, while loading a slice of pizza onto her plate. "Now, I need food first, and we'll talk shop second."

They ate multiple slices of pizza on Veronica's couch instead of in her kitchen, catching up and discussing the week they each had. The sun had set and the lighting I her living room was dim, a warm glow surrounding them as the old friends chatted casually.

"Alright, so this conference, it's your first time going, so you have no idea what kind of presentations are usually chosen?" Camilla asked, getting the background.

"Correct, I've never attended, and they no longer have last year's program listed online, so I can't even gather any historical data." Veronica replied, knowing how the gears in Camilla's brain were moving. They had been friends since college, both moving to the city after graduating. They had dreams of big city careers, trying the newest restaurants, discovering favorite hole-in-the-wall shops, and taking the train all around the city. In theory, they romanticized public transportation more than they realized. In actuality, it was unreliable at times, hot and sticky in the summer, and cold in the winter. But getting around the city with mass amounts of strangers felt a bit humanizing to Veronica. It made her feel connected to the city and the people that lived there. She appreciated all the good it brought a city, even though it could bring out the frustration in people.

"'Historical data'," Camilla repeated back to her, scoffing. Then she added lovingly, "You're such a scientist."

She looked over Veronica's application, reviewing it and tossing questions at her as they went through it. She made suggestions to change some words to make the sentences stronger, more commanding. She clarified what Veronica was trying to communicate and helped her keep the abstract succinct in some places, so she could add more content where it mattered.

"You don't have to make these changes, really. If any of this feels like it veers too far from your actual perspective, or no longer feels authentic to you - just say the word," Camilla assured her.

"Thanks, Camilla. But I feel good about all of this. I think these few changes do make it a stronger submission. I'm excited to share it with William! I just have to make sure that he has time to review it and get me edits before the deadline," Veronica said, and the presentation started to feel all the more real.

"You're going to kill it," Camilla reassured her friend.

The end of the week had arrived, and along with it was that month's staff meeting. The president of the museum would take stage in the museum's theater and present to the staff the current status of the museum, its long-term mission and short-term goals, and even the financial standing of the organization. While most of the staff had a tendency to only come for the free coffee and breakfast provided, Veronica loved a chance to check in about the museum and hear what other departments were working on.

She grabbed a coffee and settled into a seat next to William and others from the botany division.

The museum president kicked off the meeting, "I want to reiterate the museum's mission, science for all. Our mission should be in the forefront of our minds with each project we take on. How are we advancing the collections to be more accessible to scientists and researchers, both near and far? How are we making the exhibitions more approachable to audiences of all ages?"

The president finished his speech, and then handed the microphone over to the head of the Development team, who discussed a large donation the museum recently received to fund the addition of a native garden on the museum campus.

After lengthy discussions about the new garden project, the head of Development announced the latest grant awarded to the Division of Anthropology: thousands of dollars in funds were to be used to collaborate with Indigenous tribes to assist in recording and repatriating ancestral remains and cultural artifacts. The staff in the theater applauded, excited for funds that were to be used in a way that directly advances the mission of the museum.

Veronica was equally displeased at hearing the anthropology division was awarded yet another grant, as well as excited that the museum was doing its part to work closely with Indigenous tribes to return human remains and burial objects to their rightful resting places. It was important work, but she couldn't help but feel like it's just another donation made to that division, while the other research and collections within the museum stood idly by.

She scanned the staff in the seats and spotted Anthropology Collections Manager, Henry and his team from across the theater. Henry sat there with a straight face, and his glasses made his eyes look small, almost like he was constantly squinting, or judging, sizing people up.

Where William was an advocate for citizen science and sharing research with all, Henry was the complete opposite. He oversaw the anthropology collections, which included some culturally sensitive artifacts like mummies from ancient Egypt and human remains from Indigenous peoples. Part of the museum's mission was to repatriate the culturally significant items back to the people they belong to. It was important work, but Henry's demeanor was always closed off and reserved. When it came to sharing the collections, both the delicate artifacts and the sturdy ones, he acted as if the anthropology collection was to be the most protected, the most valued, and the most important.

Henry wasn't smiling, he was barely nodding his head, accepting yet another grant, another donation, another contribution. He almost seemed immune to the excitement of receiving these monetary gifts, because there were so many that came his way.

Veronica squinted at him from a distance, trying to figure him out. *Why is he the way that he is?*, she wondered. It sure wasn't his charm that was getting donors to give his division their charity.

She realized that she was staring and continued to scan the faces in the audience. Veronica recognized the new face sitting next to Henry. A face that she saw for the first time at the dismantling of the *T. rex* earlier that week. Blue Beanie Boy. But this time, he wasn't wearing his beanie, and she could see how his thick eyebrows were a perfect frame for his face. His expression mirrored Henry's, his mouth forming a straight line, unenthused. He must be a new addition to the anthropology team, which would explain why she hasn't come across him before, nor since.

The president of the museum offered the microphone to Henry, asking if he wanted to say any words, or discuss the upcoming repatriation project. Henry closed his eyes and shook his head slowly, declining the offer.

"Why is he so smug?" Veronica asked no one, under her breath. She wasn't sure if William heard her, even though he was sitting right next to her. William was a good sport about workplace venting and even downright complaining, when the right occasion called for it.

The staff meeting ended without anything else noteworthy, except Veronica's mind buzzing with additional ways she could be pushing the museum's mission forward. The main focus of her job was overseeing the volunteers in the Division of Botany, and digitizing their collection, slowly, but surely. That alone was a huge part of making their science, the research, and the collection available to all. But, Veronica was resolute, and felt like she could always do better, improve.

She ran into Henry just outside of the theater doors. Her mind oscillated between thinking about her volunteers and how they contributed to making science available to all, and seeing Henry - why couldn't volunteers do the same for other departments?

She noticed that Henry was alone, which was less intimidating, and before she could even think about it, Veronica caught up to him and put her hand lightly on his shoulder.

"Hi, Henry, can I walk with you?" she asked him, smiling to convey a working friendship.

"Sure," he uttered plainly.

Veronica wasn't sure if he recognized her, so as they walked, and to better her chances of persuasion she reminded him, "I'm Veronica, the Collections Assistant in Botany."

"Yes, yes," Henry replied quietly, but he didn't make eye contact with her, and she wasn't entirely convinced that he knew her.

"I was thinking about the museum mission, science for all, and well I oversee all of the volunteers in Botany that are digitizing our collection. It's been incredible how many specimens we have digitized for scientists to access our database across the globe."

They approached the staff elevator, and Henry swiped his badge to bring them to the staff floors where the collections were stored. "That's great," he offered, still as nonchalant as ever.

"With how popular our Anthropology collection is, what do you think about digitizing the Anthropology collection?"

Henry looked at her and quickly answered, "We don't have the manpower. We have a lot of initiatives and grants that dictate what our staff works on. It's a pipe dream, sure, but not a priority for us at the moment."

Veronica noticed he used the word "manpower" when he, in fact, had women working in anthropology too, but she brushed it off, figuring it wasn't worth dwelling on at this moment. "Yes, of course," she replied as they walked into the elevator, not willing to give up easily, "But I was thinking of volunteers. That's how we do it in Botany. It's a great opportunity for undergrad and graduate students to get hands-on experience if they are studying botany, or anthropology in your case. The thousands of visitors and even scientists across the globe that can't make it to our museum would love to access a digital collection, I'm sure of it."

It was just the two of them in the staff elevator as it lurched into motion toward the collections. Henry showed the most emotion that Veronica had ever seen him display. He scoffed, "We've never had volunteers in anthropology. Volunteers can't handle the sensitive collections."

Emotionally handle, or physically handle, she wondered what exactly he meant.

He said it succinctly, and when the elevator came to a stop on his floor, he exited toward the hallway that led to the anthropology staff offices with only a small nod as a goodbye.

The botany offices were on a different floor, and Veronica watched him walk away as the doors closed, never getting a chance to ask him to clarify, and offered a small wave goodbye that he didn't even see.

Chapter 3

Every Friday, after work for an hour or two, some the museum staff would meet in one of the classrooms on the staff-only floor for a casual "happy hour". The event itself was spread through word-of-mouth, and never written about formally since it wasn't exactly a sanctioned gathering, but museum directors turned a blind eye being that it never got out of hand.

Classroom B saw the same regulars each week on Friday at 4:30 PM, but newcomers would come and go. Everyone could sign up to bring beverages to share, or snacks. Veronica's boss was a Classroom B Happy Hour regular; some would even consider William the mayor of Happy Hour. Each week he ensured that drinks were stocked and that the snacks sign up list was passed around. Like the proponent for science that he was, he was also a proponent for scientists networking with each other. He always said that the exchanging of ideas happened in the lab, the collections, the field, and in the bar.

Feeling celebratory after having finished her presentation abstract, the only next step was for William to review it, Veronica tagged along with him this week and headed to Classroom B. Following his lead, she dropped a couple of dollars into the donation bucket to cover the cost of her beer, grabbed a can of a local Midwest beer from the cooler filled that was with ice and cold beverages, and she popped open the top.

Like in many happy hour situations, there is always the half-second pause that happens right after getting a beverage, but right before finding someone to talk to. Veronica's eyes darted to William instinctually, but he was already speaking to Henry. Henry stood there with a slight frown on his face. He wasn't a tall man, but he looked especially short next to the tall man standing next to him: the new face she kept seeing at the museum. She couldn't help but notice the Blue Beanie Boy, and how the waves in his hair caught the warm light of Classroom B. Gold strands speckled throughout his dark hair stood out like a halo. He was good looking, despite the fact that he hadn't smiled and wore a straight face like Henry every time she saw him. This was the closest she had been to him since she first noticed him, and his height commanded a presence. Veronica equally felt herself drawn to him, and wanting to run from him at the same time.

Just as Veronica decided to turn to find someone else to talk to, William caught her eyes and called her over. She begrudgingly approached the small group and William already began his introduction, "Veronica, Henry has a new visiting researcher. He'll be working on preservation in their division."

"Nice to meet you, I'm Artie," Blue Beanie Boy introduced himself and gave a forced, polite smile and an outstretched hand. He had dark features, but his eyes seemed bright, even in the dusty classroom light.

"Nice to meet you too," Veronica replied, shaking his warm hand, and hoping to not come off too friendly and get caught spending the next hour speaking with Henry.

William, the social butterfly that he was, chimed in immediately with, "Veronica Sterling is the Collections Assistant in Botany with me. She heads up digitizing our collections and oversees all of our volunteers."

Artie replied with a quick, "Nice." Although his reply was short, almost curt, he had a small smile with his response and he confidently held eye contact, until he didn't. Veronica tried to get a read on him; did his prolonged eye contact make her nervous? Or did it make her excited?

Curiosity getting the best of her and realizing she hadn't seen him around before these last few days, she asked, "How long ago did you start?"

"This is my first week," Artie replied, taking a sip of his beer.

"This is your first week and you're already coming to staff happy hour?" William cried in disbelief, impressed with any scientist that was social by choice, like himself.

"Arturo is a postdoc and has been awarded the visiting scientist fellowship to spend time here learning about our preservation techniques, and will be writing a paper on the work." Henry chimed in, using Artie's formal name, Veronica supposed. She wanted to roll her eyes at Henry taking every opportunity to mention every grant and gift that the anthropology division benefitted from. Everything Henry said sounded flat, uninspired and yet boastful at the same time. Veronica felt lucky to work under William, who made every scientist sound like a celebrity, and every research project sound like the greatest discovery.

"Did you get your PhD at the university campus downtown?" William asked Artie; he was great at engaging people almost as if he was interviewing them.

"Yes, I've lived in the city for a while now," Artie replied succinctly, somewhat vague and reserved.

Is he a mini Henry? Veronica wondered. *Just what museums need: another scientist making museums seem unapproachable and elitist.*

A pause in the conversation almost gave her a chance to give the group her pleasantries and find others to talk to, but before she could, a colleague that works as a fossil preparator stepped up to William to share, "Hey William, we're out of beer."

"On it. Veronica, I could use a hand carrying some cases back here," William went into Happy Hour Mayor mode, and turned to Veronica, and then to Artie. "Artie, if you want everyone to like you starting your first week, come help and walk in here with more beer."

William's cool was contagious; he could effortlessly make anyone feel like the most important person in the room. Being that he was one of the longest employees of the museum, he knew everyone, and had a charm about him. It was hard to say no to any of his requests, and Veronica watched Artie fall under his spell.

The three of them took the staff elevator to the floor where the liquor was locked up. William unlocked the storage room and handed a case of beer into each of their outstretched arms. They each carried a case back onto the elevator, and while they made small talk, Veronica couldn't help but notice glances from Artie.

"So what did you think of your first week? Do you like it so far?" she asked Artie, trying to pry more out of him, willing him to not be a mute clone of Henry.

"I've learned a lot already, but there's still so much to learn," he replied vaguely.

Cheekily, William urged him on, "First lesson in staff happy hour, you walk in first carrying the beer."

The elevator doors opened just outside of Classroom B, and when Artie walked into the room holding his case of beer in front of him, the museum staff let out cheers.

Two staff members from the fossil prep lab, Akira and Ben, approached to help set the additional beer on ice in the coolers. Although Veronica never spent too much working time with them, she saw them regularly at happy hour each week, and they always greeted her warmly and offered to help William with any prep he needed to keep weekly happy hour going.

"Have you met Artie already?" Veronica asked them, motioning to the quiet presence to her right once they finished setting out the beer.

"Briefly, at the staff meeting earlier this week," Akira shared.

"It's good to see you at happy hour already," Ben added.

Artie nodded, remaining quiet as they each helped themselves to a second round. They tapped their cans of beer together casually and said "cheers" in unison.

"Alright, how do we get to know the newest team member?" Akira asked the group, wearing her excitement on her face.

"You mean, like an icebreaker?" Ben questioned.

"Yeah, like two truths and a lie," Akira replied before taking a sip from her beer.

"Well, let's do that," Veronica agreed to it, compliance seeming like the easiest answer. She noticed that Artie hadn't spoken much besides the introductions.

"I can go first, give all of you time to think of something," Ben offered kindly. Maybe he also sensed that the newest fellow needed some time to warm up. "Alright, here's my three - I'm a night owl, I collect old radios, and I'm a vegetarian."

"I've worked with you so long, I think it's unfair for me to guess first," Akira laughed.

"Let me think," Veronica eyed Ben, "Is the lie that you're a vegetarian?"

"I think the lie is that you're a night owl," Akira offered.

"You do know me too well," Ben confirmed that Akira was right.

"Yeah, I'm more likely to run into you before the sunrise, not after sunset, especially when out in the field!" Akira surmised, continuing, "Alright, alright. You have to sit mine out. Let's see, I went to boarding school, I've been to fifteen countries, and I'm double jointed."

After a long pause, realizing that Ben and Artie were not going to offer up anything, Veronica went for it, "Did you not go to boarding school?"

"I did go to boarding school! Other guesses?" Akira

"Process of elimination, I'm going to say that you are not double jointed. You've traveled a lot," Ben said, unsure.

"I have actually only been to eight countries, if you can believe it. Mostly for dig sites," Akira clarified.

The group nodded in understanding, waiting for the next person to continue their happy hour game. Veronica sensed that Artie was still quiet at her side.

"Well, I'll go. My three - I'm a dog person, I'm a picky eater, and I love the winter," Veronica eyed their faces as she spoke, looking for traces of them catching her in the lie.

"Is the fact that you're a picky eater a lie?" Artie asked Veronica almost immediately, holding eye contact with her for the first time.

She was surprised, he guessed it right pretty quickly, "Yeah, am I that easy to read?"

"I can't believe you love the winter. You are a true Midwesterner," Akira remarked.

"Listen, I'm not the only winter lover. William's favorite season is winter too, so I'm not completely mad," Veronica defended.

"You two are in the minority, I'm sure. Alright, Artie, you're up," Akira pointed a finger at him.

"Let's see. I am a dual citizen, I move around a lot, and I once met Jane Goodall in an elevator," Artie said. Veronica's eyes went wide. The Jane Goodall one was specific enough that it could be true, or it could be the wildcard of a lie.

"Okay, this is just a wild guess considering we just met you. But I'm going to say you aren't a dual citizen," Akira guessed, her voice raising an octave at the end as if in question.

"The lie is that I move around a lot. I was born and raised here, I've lived in the city all my life," Artie clarified, not giving time for either Ben or Veronica to guess. Veronica wasn't sure if he said it with pride, or with remorse.

"You really met Jane Goodall?" Veronica asked, incredulously. "I adore her."

"Yeah, she was in town for an interview at my university. It made my week."

"The best elevator ride ever. What was she like?" Veronica gushed.

"As kind in person as she seems in interviews," he replied, his gaze not leaving her wide eyes.

"Alright, that was a good one to end on. Now, it's late, I better get going," Ben stated, eyeing the clock on the wall. Veronica was surprised to see that it had been nearly two hours that they had been there. She never closed out happy hour before; she always aimed to make it to her train before the sun set.

"It's late for you, but you're right, happy hour is coming to an end," Akira replied, looking around at the thin crowd. "Artie, nice to get to know you a bit more, and I'm sure we'll be running into you again. Don't be a stranger."

They said their goodbyes, and Veronica stopped by her office to grab her coat and her bag before making the walk across the museum campus to catch the night train. The pedestrian path to the closest train station was lit, but the night sky was dark enough for her eyes to have to strain to see.

As she walked, she watched the city skyline jut out at various heights on the horizon in front of her. Each building's lights peeked out from their windows, twinkling like stars against the darkness.

It would be one of the last times she had to make the post-happy hour walk in the dark to the train, alone.

Veronica and Camilla met up that weekend for hotdogs and fries at their favorite street vendor, paired with a viewing of one of Veronica's favorite old movies.

"What movie are we going to see again?" Camilla asked, her teeth snapping her hotdog, pickle, and sport peppers with a crunch.

"The old theater is playing A Streetcar Named Desire. Remember? Street food cart dinner paired with a street car movie?" Veronica offered, knowing Camilla loved a theme.

"Isn't that movie problematic?" her friend asked, dipping a fry in ketchup.

"Aren't most old films problematic? They're playing it in 35mm."

"Is that special?" Camilla asked innocently while chewing on some fries.

"Marlon Brando looks the best he's ever looked in it," Veronica tried a different approach to convince her friend it was worth it.

"The Godfather?"

"Yes, but young."

Camilla said nothing but offered a compliant expression, and Veronica excitedly dipped three fries in the ketchup.

The theater was small, with an old market light marquee outside that blinked to illuminate the current title playing on its single screen. Veronica and Camilla purchased their tickets at the ticket booth outside, and then waited in the small theater lobby to get popcorn.

It was their turn to order and Camilla asked the cashier for a large popcorn to share, when Veronica saw a familiar face through the other side of the window glass. Beyond Camilla's shoulder, Veronica's eyes somehow focused on his face, among all of the faces in the distance.

Artie was waiting in line, outside the theater to buy tickets with someone she didn't recognize. A tall woman, with smooth, dark hair that looked like it fell effortlessly past her shoulders with just the right amount of bounce. As someone who had to work to tame her own dense waves into something smooth and beautiful, Veronica found jealousy in the pit of her stomach.

But why? She just met him, and while she found him attractive and found herself wanting to get him to open up to her, she felt that her feelings of jealousy were out of left field, and she did her best to push them away.

Camilla treated them to popcorn since Veronica bought the movie tickets. The swipe of her credit card brought Veronica back to the present moment. She dropped her eyes from staring at Artie in the distance, and focused softly on the art deco carpet under her feet.

"Can we sit in the back? I don't love having to crane my neck," Camilla requested as she walked toward the theater to find a seat.

Veronica absent-mindedly agreed and followed her friend while lost in her own thoughts. She mindlessly watched the movie and snacked on the large bucket of popcorn that Camilla propped on the armrest between them. It was a movie that Veronica had seen dozens of times, but she was having a hard time letting herself get lost in the silver screen.

The end credits started rolling, when Camilla enthusiastically jumped up, wanting to beat the crowd to the exit.

Veronica realized she was in and out of the theater without Artie catching sight of her, but she couldn't help but notice him, and his companion from a distance. She felt socially awkward, knowing that if it was Camilla that recognized someone that she thought was cute, she would have gone up to say hi confidently.

When they had entered the theater, it was still light outside, albeit a little gray with clouds blocking the sun. But now that the movie was over, the sun had set and instead of walking to the train in the dark, Veronica and her friend decided to split a ride-share back to their separate homes.

They waited outside the front of the theater doors, their faces illuminated brightly by the blinking marquee above them. Camilla muttered something about a black Prius being three minutes away, but Veronica barely registered it when she clocked the newly familiar voice behind her. Low and warm, it had a hint of an accent with a sing-song quality. To Veronica, it was unmistakable.

"Listen, I have an idea of how to court someone," she heard him say.

"Oh, sure," his companion replied, and it sounded like she was teasing him.

"Just give me time, you'll see," was all Veronica heard him say before his voice trailed off as the two walked farther away, leaving the front of the theater for their own car or train ride to take them away.

Chapter 4

It was the start to another week, and the city's spring still had a chill in the air cold enough for Veronica to opt for the train instead of biking to work. Public transit at peak commute times wasn't the most comfortable ride, but Veronica had gotten used to the tight quarters and rocky ride.

As soon as she stepped foot inside the museum, the building's main hall opened to an atrium with skylights and a ceiling nearly 100 feet above her head. All that space more than made up for a ride in a packed train car to get there.

First agenda item for the day was her weekly meeting with William. William had an office, but was so rarely in it. This time, the first place Veronica checked to find him was the botany collections. The herbarium was long, with a counter spanning entirely down one side, with chairs for people to sit and work on specimens, and everything else they needed at their fingertips to study the specimens including research journals, field notebooks, herbarium mounting papers, and specimen labels.

Veronica found William exactly where she expected him, at one of the computers along the counters.

"Good morning," she called out to him.

William shot a glance her way and motioned her to pull up a chair, "Morning, sit, sit."

Veronica slid an old chair closer to where William sat. After discussing their weekends, William got right into discussing the presentation that she sent to him for review.

"Content is great, I honestly don't have any feedback on your title or abstract. It sounds like a great presentation on the work that you do here. The only thing I could help with is maybe giving you some background on the conference itself, and maybe help you prepare for the actual speaking part," William explained with his easy-going nature.

"That would be great. Do you really think it'll be accepted?" Veronica asked, tensing, unsure of the response she was about to hear.

"I have attended many times and presented a symposium a few times too. From my experience, innovative topics are the ones that tend to be accepted. Digitizing the collections, finding a way to bridge the gap between different museum collections, various collection management systems, this is all useful work that once presented to other institutions, we can only hope it will inspire them to implement the process you've built."

"Right, it truly benefits the entire scientific community when we are all working together, collection sharing."

"You're going to be great. You should send it before the end of day. Now, when it comes to physically standing on a stage in front of people, how comfortable are you?"

"Truthfully? I'll probably have a stomachache for days before it actually happens," Veronica replied, and she could already feel her stomach dropping as if she was on a rollercoaster.

"Sounds like we should get you practicing in front of some people. Start with someone you're comfortable with, like a friend. See how it goes," he encouraged.

Veronica nodded slowly and took a deep breath. Presenting at the conference all sounded good in theory. Once she sent it off to the conference organizers for their review of her submission, if it was accepted, that was it, it would all become even more real. Her stomach was dropping again.

"So you'll submit your presentation today?' William asked, sensing her nerves.

"Yes, of course," she responded, convincing herself, too.

"What else is priority this week for you? We have the off-site event that you're spearheading this week. Do you need any support from me?" William instinctively put his glasses on, low on his nose, and grabbed a notebook and pencil, ready to jot down action items for himself.

"I was thinking of bringing some of the economic botany specimens for this pop-up event. Particularly, the ethnobotanical specimens."

"Sounds good, since you'll be the one onsite and your specialty is neotropical biology, I think that makes the most sense. Will you be bringing any of the volunteers?"

"Of course, two have signed up to be at the display with me, engaging with attendees. I figure with three of us, that gives each of us a chance to break as needed."

"Great plan. Anything else you need? Help with bringing the specimens there? Setting up or breaking down?"

"William, I appreciate your offer, but really, we can handle it," Veronica reassured him.

"I know you can handle it, but I'm also here to help with the grunt work, not just the glamorous parts," he offered with a smile, looking at her over the glasses that slipped further and further down his nose.

"I appreciate that, and I'll let you know if one of the volunteers suddenly can't make it, but otherwise, we've got it covered."

"Good plan," William replied, taking his glasses off and putting them on a stack of binders next to the computer.

"Don't think that gets you out of our annual behind the scenes night. We definitely can't do that without you," Veronica said with a hint of fear.

"I wouldn't dream of missing my favorite event of the year."

Chapter 5

Veronica was prepping her botany volunteers for an off-site event that was taking place downtown. The division of botany and other collections departments in the museum were bringing actual artifacts and specimens out of the museum, and into the pop-up event to promote the latest renovation of one of the museum halls.

She scheduled the volunteers to support the event in shifts, each tackling a different responsibility. There was a display of ethnobotanical specimens, how people use plants, that Veronica planned to use as conversation starters with attendees. The main activity of the botany section were fresh plant specimens and showing attendees how to press the plants themselves and make proper labels, their very own personal botany collections. Veronica had a volunteer handling the sign-ups for the activity, the other volunteer managing inventory of the plants and flowers for pressing, and she planned to do the hands-on pressing with event attendees herself, with each of them rotating and taking breaks as needed.

Onsite, she arrived with boxes of supplies for the event, and started setting up as her volunteers and other museum staff trickled in. The event was in a historic building downtown that used to be an old athletic club. The building had been boarded up for decades, and when investors purchased it to convert it to a hotel, they found intricate wooden details on each floor, an old indoor pool with the tiles still intact, and even an old basketball court, though the shine on the floors was long-gone. The renovations were carefully carried out to keep the integrity of the original details, and even replicas were made for the architectural details that couldn't be salvaged.

The beauty of the old building surrounding her reminded Veronica of the intricate architecture of her museum, as well. She set up the botany section and could see the different division sections setting up their own areas with interesting artifacts and specimens. The staff paleontologists set up fossils that people could touch on tables, and fossils behind glass were set up at a distance. The Collections Manager of the insects division was setting up an insect-pinning activity, which was sure to be popular. Spread all around her table were butterfly, moth, and beetle specimens, waiting to be mounted and displayed.

Scanning the room, Veronica noticed one division was missing - anthropology. As she finished setting up, she huffed to herself, not surprised. Soon enough, the start time of the event approached, and the event team opened the doors. Attendees came in and dispersed to various areas: the bar for drinks, the lounge areas for a seat, to the volunteers with clip-boards to sign up for activities, and to the many tables representing the different scientific collections of the museum.

Once the event began, the room filled with a lively chatter, and Veronica found herself talking to her volunteers that had questions, saying hello to fellow staff members that were networking, and conversing with attendees that had a spark in their eyes, pleased to experience the collections in a new way.

When there was only an hour left of the event, the room calmed down enough for her to take a seat in the nearest sitting area. She grabbed a spot on the couch, within view of the botany volunteers, in case they needed anything. A bartender approached, offering her a drink, and Veronica gladly accepted a glass of ice water, needing to quench her thirst after hours of talking.

The bartender delivered her drink, and as he walked away, behind him stood a handsome man. She did a double-take, and then realized it was Artie, speaking with two of the museum's fossil preparators, Akira and Ben. Veronica considered that he must be opening up and making friends at the museum, remembering how when she spent time with him at happy hour, he seemed quite reserved.

She found herself admiring how striking his body looked in the dim event lighting; his skin picked up the warmth of the soft bulb lights, and the blues and reds from the up lights created a halo around him.

As if he could sense her eyes on him, he turned her way and barely waited a beat before smiling and leaving his group to approach her.

"I'm surprised you're here, since Henry isn't," Veronica said to Artie, as he sat next to her on the couch.

"I wanted to support the museum," he replied simply, placing his drink next to Veronica's on the low table in front of them. She turned toward him and nearly gushed. He really did look warm and attractive in the glow of the moody event space.

Catching herself, she processed what he was saying. Anyone that believed in the museum's mission enough to show up simply to support the cause, surely, they couldn't be all that self-important, like Henry. But at the same time, Artie was so reserved, and when he did speak, his mannerisms reminded her of his research sponsor, and she couldn't quite shake that.

Veronica realized she was staring and blinked to bring herself out of her own thoughts, "Well I'm glad you're here. Have you met most of the staff?"

"Akira and Ben have been very welcoming. The fossil collection is right next to anthropology's large storage area." Artie shared.

"How come there's no section for anthropology tonight? I know you can't bring some of our bronze sculptures or Indigenous canoes to this pop-up, but surely some of our smaller artifacts could be brought out for the attendees?" Veronica teased him, hoping to make him comfortable enough to share why anthropology was the only collection not represented tonight.

Artie seemed to hold back a smile, while solemnly sharing, "Henry is very protective of the collection and preserving the artifacts. Each time one is transported and handled, it deteriorates their integrity." He spoke admiringly about his research sponsor, showing respect. "I'm sure some of the collection isn't too delicate to transport and share, carefully, with attendees. But Henry wasn't having it."

Veronica nodded understandingly, and they both looked at their drinks on the table. *That sure did sound like Henry*, she thought.

Before Veronica could think of anything to add, Artie clarified his standpoint, "I feel too new to the museum to change his mind."

Maybe in his short time working in the anthropology collection he could be the change they needed. Feeling hopeful, Veronica gave it a shot.

"Preservation is important - but why couldn't the collection be digitized in the meantime? Sure, an Indigenous canoe can only be photographed and shared online on a small scale compared to studying the artifact in person, but it could show useful historical data, if the artifact itself were to deteriorate over time despite preservation efforts." She looked at him wide eyed, suddenly realizing how passionate she sounded about it.

Looking back to her, he softened and replied kindly, "You're right. I think that it would be amazing to be able to share the artifacts we have digitally, or in whatever form we could in the short term. Not everyone can visit the museum to see the collections that are on display. Hell, not everyone is awarded the visiting scientist fellowship to study particular artifacts that might be pertinent to their research."

She felt his passion for science mirroring her own. It felt good. It felt *so* good to be seen and heard. And then -

"But Henry is a bit old school. His perspective is that the anthropology collection holds some culturally sensitive items, and we can't be so quick to share them. Especially without consulting representatives from each culture that they belong to..." he replied quietly, seeming to trail off.

"And you don't think you could persuade Henry otherwise? I'm sure there are examples of other institutions handling sensitive collections digitally," she asked, trying to catch his eyes.

He grabbed his drink to take a sip, but before he did, he murmured, hopefully, "Maybe, in time."

The event began to wrap up, so they casually said goodbye and Artie joined the paleontology division to help them pack up the collection items that they brought. The botany volunteers and Veronica made quick work of their breakdown. That was the one benefit of managing a collection that is lightweight and each object the size of a letter.

As she walked to the exit, Veronica tried to catch Artie's eyes, but he was deep in clean up mode with the fossil prep lab team. She left, still thinking about their conversation, and pleased with getting him to open up a bit more. She hadn't felt this good after a conversation in a long time.

Chapter 6

Veronica couldn't tell you when the first flower arrived at her office. It wasn't a floral arrangement in a vase with a note. Instead, someone sent her, a botanist that oversaw an entire collection of pressed specimens in a museum, a pressed flower. She found the flower in the interoffice mailbox on the wall just outside of her office door, propped up gently in front of the rest of her mail at the museum. It was a somewhat recently cut flower, the petals soft, the color of the stem and leaves a fresh green. The specimen was not faded or brittle like the ones the collection housed within the museum, like her own childhood collection at home.

This specimen was a violet, small and purple. Unlike a proper collected specimen, it included very little information on the label. It noted the genus and species in a pretty, italicized font, but not where it was collected or when. A simple, "*Viola sororia.*" From a museum collection perspective, it was somewhat useless without pertinent information to link it to a time and place, and who collected it. From a personal perspective, it was beautiful and dainty, the color of the petals so rich it looked like it might stain the paper.

After a weekly staff meeting, Veronica caught up to William to walk back to the botany division together. Once their steps were in line, she asked, "Did you put the unlabeled specimen in my mailbox? The violet flower?"

"No," he stated simply, looking at her sideways with a glance that said, *go on.*

"Do you know who it could be from? There's no collection data on the label. It's surprising there is a label at all," she probed, as they passed office after office, walking through the dim staff-only hallways.

"Perhaps one of the volunteers found it in the collection and wasn't sure what to do with the unlabeled specimen?" William offered before departing for another meeting in a different direction, which left Veronica walking solo back to the botany collection.

It didn't seem likely that a volunteer would place the specimen in her mailbox without so much as a note or an email about it. She made a mental note to ask a few of the volunteers if they might know anything about it next time she saw them.

Part Two

Daisy

Chapter 7

Veronica plopped down next to Frances at the long, boardroom table for the museum's Diversity, Equity, and Inclusion Committee meeting. The museum leadership recruited various staff to fill roles for the committee, with the hopes that representation from the collections, administrative roles, and even front of house positions would bring a wider variety of insights to the museum's DEI efforts.

After some small talk amongst the committee members, the lead kicked it off. "Applications for the summer internships are opening soon. So, the main discussion for this week's meeting is if we will open up the internships to applicants outside of the city for the first time."

"Doesn't opening it up allow for a more diverse pool of candidates?" a colleague from the gift shop asked.

The lead shook her head thoughtfully before responding, "At a glance, you would think so. But if we were to accept interns from all over the country, we would inadvertently be opening up the internship to applicants that can afford to live in a city that they aren't local to, all summer. I'm not sure that applicants that can afford temporary housing for months on end exactly *need* an opportunity like an internship at a large institution."

"In theory, it could give us more diverse candidates geographically, but not socioeconomically," Frances chimed in.

"Exactly. The thinking being that if someone is well off enough that they could afford to rent outside of their home base for the summer, they likely have other opportunities for their resumes."

"So, it's a matter of getting some locals who are not as fortunate to get a leg up with their own resumes and experience."

"Precisely."

In the end, the consensus was to leave the summer internship as-is, and only keep it available to locals.

Dividing and conquering, Veronica's task was to collect the descriptions of each internship role from various departments, and then Frances was going to manage the application process.

When the meeting was done, Frances asked Veronica if she had time for a coffee to discuss how the process went last year.

They made their way together to the museum's cafe and ordered two coffees. They took a seat in the cafe, underneath a life-size model of a flying pterosaur. The soft roar of the museum attendees echoed in the expansive museum hall around them.

"So," Frances started as she sipped her coffee, "What worked well, and what didn't work well, with the intern application process last year?"

Veronica shook her head, "The first year the DEI internships were piloted, we only involved HR toward the end of the process. We learned from that mistake, and now we involve them from the beginning. Once I collect all of the different department projects that each intern will be working on, you'll work with Heidi in HR to get them on the website. Heidi will also get them setup on our payroll system once applicants are chosen. But you'll be the interns main contact for the museum, their go-to person. Kind of like their buddy for all things museum related."

Frances was taking notes and nodding her head.

Veronica continued, "The museum has so many different internships and opportunities, it's hard to keep them all straight. But we realized last year that we didn't have to reinvent the wheel, we can streamline the process like other departments have."

"So you're the main point of contact for all of the different departments that are bringing on an intern for the summer, and I'm the main point of contact for the interns themselves?" Frances summarized.

"Exactly," Veronica affirmed with a satisfying sip of her coffee.

"Got it. With all of the museum's different programs, we get to meet so many people; this new cohort of interns, the visiting scientists each year, even our different lab research experiences for undergraduates," Frances said thoughtfully, her pen stopping at the end of her notes.

"Yeah," was all Veronica said. Her mind immediately fixated on this year's visiting scientist. She found herself lost in her thoughts of how she felt when she saw Artie last, at the pop-up event. He had opened up to her a little bit that night, and it left her wanting to know more. He had shared a little bit of Henry's reasoning and perspective, and yet, she wanted to know more about Artie's point of view.

She was brought back to the present, sitting there with Frances and their coffees, and she suddenly felt quintessential butterflies in her stomach. She hadn't felt that feeling in a long time, and yet she knew exactly what it meant. The last couple of times she had feelings for someone, she got hurt.

"Where did you go?" Frances said, giggling at Veronica's faraway look.

Veronica blinked, and took a breath to push her nerves away, then replied, "No where I want to revisit."

❋

It was a typical end of the week where Veronica was wrapping up her day with the last of her meetings. She left a staff meeting, and instinctively checked emails on her phone to parse through spam and emails without action items.

As she mindlessly archived spam emails, she came upon an email from the Association of Natural History Collections Forum (ANHCF) regarding an update about her submitted presentation.

Veronica let out an unexpected gasp as her eyes quickly scanned the first few sentences for a status update. And then she saw it.

> Your submission, *Expanding access and usage of natural history collections through digitization*, has been accepted to the Association of Natural History Collections Forum program. We look forward to having you participate in this upcoming conference and presenting your work. The conference will take place in San Francisco, California from...

She stopped reading at that point, figuring she would have time to digest the details of the email later. In this moment, she felt so excited she could squeal, and immediately felt the need to find William to tell him, so she headed to the herbarium.

Veronica found William standing in the botany collection, muttering to himself as he compared notes in a binder to specimens on a shelf in the economic botany aisle.

"William, can I interrupt?" Veronica asked, gauging how deep his concentration was.

He looked up from the binder in his hands, his eyes peering out from above his glasses that always slipped to the end of his nose. "Go for it," he said.

"My submission was accepted to the conference," she blurted out.

William slammed the binder shut with one hand, and a puff of dust escaped from between the pages, almost like a confetti cannon was congratulating her.

"That's fantastic," he beamed. "We've got some work to do to prepare in the short time frame. But for now, you should celebrate, I hope?"

"Yes, but I just had to tell you!"

"Congratulations, your first presentation. It's going to be great; I assure you. Take the weekend to celebrate, and let's tackle the presentation slides next week. Sound like a plan?"

Veronica nodded excitedly. She was buzzing with so much excitement that even the nervous part of her was quieted down.

She walked back to her office with excitement in her step and took out her phone to text Camilla and her parents that her submission was accepted.

CAMILLA: *Woohoo congrats! Drinks on me this weekend to celebrate!*

MOM: *That's wonderful news, congrats! When are you coming home to visit? You should come one weekend and tell us all about it. Just let me know when and what you request for dinner xo*

Veronica's mind started mentally scrolling through her calendar to map out a weekend she could make the trek to the suburbs to visit her parents. One thing she did know, she was definitely free to get drinks with Camilla.

Veronica popped out of the train station with a burst of her umbrella to protect herself from the downpour of rain as she made her way to the dive bar to meet her friend.

Just a few blocks later she was ducking into the warm entrance of a cozy dive bar. She closed the umbrella, shaking it off on the mat, and her black ankle boots had kept the city puddles out of her socks. The dive bar had Christmas lights hung around the bar, year-round, and a jukebox in the corner that actually worked, playing 80's darkwave. Veronica didn't have to look around long to know that her friend was there, she knew her well enough to know she must have chosen this music.

Veronica took a seat at the bar next to Camilla, giving a side hug as they said hello.

"Do you go to any other bars?" Veronica teased her friend, knowing this was her spot.

"Listen, this is one of the few dive bars with an acceptable bathroom that is closest to the train. Kind of important in this kind of weather," Camilla cried, pointing to the small front windows streaked with raindrops.

"We have two very different definitions of acceptable bathrooms," Veronica gave a small laugh as she dug in her purse for actual dollar bills for the cash only bar.

"It's clean!" her friend defended.

"But it doesn't lock!" Veronica rebutted.

Camilla rolled her eyes, "Put your money away. I've got this round. As a congratulations to your first submission being accepted to a scientific conference."

Camilla caught the bartender's attention to order, and as he approached, Veronica admired how handsome he was. It took a moment, but she looked away when she realized who the dark haired, brooding bartender reminded her of.

They ordered their drinks, and when they arrived, they tapped them together, followed by a tap of their drinks to the bar top before they each took a sip.

"Cheers, and thanks for the drink," Veronica said to her friend.

"Cheers! And truth be told, my motives for treating you to a round may not just be to celebrate your presentation," Camilla looked like she was in pain, her mouth a forced smile.

"What is it?"

"Just a favor."

"Yes, I gathered that. What's the favor?" Veronica stared at her friend suspiciously.

"I need your help moving," before Veronica could protest, Camilla added, "I have movers doing the big stuff, but the valuables, the stuff I'll need the night before and morning of, I'm going to box up and bring over in a ride-share. I could use an extra hand."

"Oh, that's all?"

"Yes. Moving is annoying, I know -"

"Camilla, it's no sweat. That's what friends are for. When's the move?"

"In a few weeks, after you're back from the conference."

"You've got it, count me in."

"Well, that was too easy, thank you," Camilla smiled at Veronica.

There was a comfortable back and forth cadence to their conversation, and Veronica caught the eyes of the bartender, before he looked down at their drinks, sizing up if she and Camilla were ready for another round. Veronica's mind had drifted to the conference, and to thinking about work. And with that, a particular someone at work.

"Remember that museum pop-up event I told you I was participating in?" Veronica asked, trying to sound effortless.

"Vaguely. You do so many events at the museum," Camilla narrowed her eyes, trying to remember.

"This one actually wasn't at the museum at all, it was a pop-up at a historic building downtown," Veronica clarified, trying to jog her friend's memory.

"Oh yeah, how did it go?"

"Great! It was a good turn out for a weeknight. Nearly every museum department was represented."

"Love to hear that. I'll try to come to the next one."

"You should. There's this new postdoc fellow, in anthropology. I met him at museum happy hour," Veronica didn't make eye contact with her friend, but she felt her eyes on her.

"Oh? This new postdoc fellow? Met him at happy hour... And?"

Veronica glanced at her friend, "He's kind of a closed book, but I find myself wanting to pry him open."

"And he's really good looking?"

"So good looking," Veronica practically burst.

Camilla laughed, "Well look at you. I'm glad you've got someone you're interested in. It's been a while, huh?"

Veronica knew her friend couldn't help but notice the long lapse in time since her last two relationships. "Yeah, well, aside from all the regular risks that come with having feelings for someone and letting the person know, there's even more risks with this. We work together," Veronica sighed.

Camilla gave her friend a knowing look, "Listen, I'm not going to push you. I know you'll open yourself up to someone again when the time is right for you. But don't you think it might be time that the risk might be worth it?"

Veronica stared at her hands around her drink and said simply, "Maybe."

Camilla had known Veronica long enough to know when she no longer wanted to talk about a subject. "Want to see my inspiration for how I'm going to decorate my new apartment?"

Veronica lit up, appreciating the comfort of a long-term friend. "Absolutely," she beamed.

Chapter 8

Veronica was looking forward to the staff happy hour this week. Her presentation was accepted to the scientific conference, and she was feeling the support from all around - William, her friends, her family. Also, after bumping into Artie at the museum pop-up event, she was hoping he'd make it back to Classroom B so that she could continue talking to him. She didn't wait for William to finish up in the Botany division before she headed that way at 4:30 PM sharp. She turned her computer off, and put the plant specimens that were on her desk back into their appropriate collections cabinets before heading to the comforting dustiness of Classroom B.

She paid her dues, grabbed a beer, snacked on some veggies and hummus and was chatting with Frances among the various dips on the table in between them. At the same time, she was glancing over her shoulder to the door to see who was entering every time someone new arrived. Frances worked in the PR department and was another advocate for sharing science across the world. It was essentially her job to ensure the museum collections were known and used globally, but it was also a passion of hers to boast about the museum's research and collections on a regular basis. They shared that enthusiasm, and Veronica always found her positive attitude pleasant, and her candid banter refreshing.

Deep in an amusing discussion about what kind of animals they each saw themselves as, Veronica sensed a presence to her right, and when she turned, she was pleased to see the tanned skin, eyes the color of honey, and big smile of Artie, right next to her.

She reflected his grin right back at him and simply said, "Hi."

"Hi, good to see you," he lifted his beer up to hers to tap them together.

"Cheers," she declared, touching the bottom of her beer to his while he continued to smile. He casually licked his bottom lip and took a sip of his beer. The motion of his jaw clenching dazed her, and she searched for anything to say. "Do you know Frances? She works in the PR department."

"No, I don't. Pleasure, I'm Artie," he quickly turned his body away from Veronica and extended his hand to introduce himself to Frances, his smile fading.

Frances dropped the baby carrot she was just about to bite onto her plate, wiped her hand dramatically before shaking his and said, "I'm Frances, nice to meet you too. You're working with Henry on your research, right?"

"Yes," he responded, each of them returning their hands to their sides. "Part of my postdoc fellowship, I'm focusing on preservation techniques." Again, he shared limited information, and it left Veronica with a longing of wanting to know what interested him about preservation, about anthropology. At that moment, she wanted to know a whole lot more about him than just his work. She wanted to know if he was a morning lark or a night owl, how he took his coffee, if he was right or left-handed.

Before she got a chance to ask any follow up questions about his fellowship, Frances went right back into the discussion they were having. She turned to Veronica and said, "I could definitely see you as a beetle."

Veronica grinned, pleased, adding, "Right? Beetles spend their days in the dirt, hiding under various plants. Seems like me in a nutshell."

Getting a few laughs, Veronica pressed on, fixing on Artie to bring him up to speed and into the conversation, "Frances sees herself as an owl, like how in fantasy books and movies the owl is the one that brings letters and mail. Somewhat of a communicator in the animal kingdom, being the science communicator that she is." Frances confidently held her hands out and looked around, putting herself on display. Chuckling at her confidence, Veronica went on,

"What about you, Artie? What kind of animal do you see yourself as?"

"Me?" Artie asked, motioning to himself before putting a hand in his pocket. He stared off, thoughtfully. "I'm a fox. They're curious, adaptable to any environment, and can be aggressive." He looked pleased with himself.

"That's a pretty good one!" Frances exclaimed.

Veronica looked at him sideways. Most scientists, by nature, are curious. But adaptable and aggressive? That sounded a little alarming and untrustworthy.

Frances and Artie spoke a little, and others came and went from the group, a casual rotation of rubbing elbows with fellow staff members that they may not interact with all the time.

While Veronica was in discussion with Artie and various staff members, Jane from the museum events team came up to her, calling her name.

"Veronica! I heard from William that your presentation was accepted at ANHCF. Congrats!" Jane held up her drink, miming cheers.

"Thank you, thank you. It's my first time at the event, so we'll see how well it goes," Veronica was equally appreciative of the support from her fellow staff member, but also a little embarrassed at the attention. Scientists' presentations were accepted all the time, talks were given every year, and life moved on.

"You'll be speaking at ANHCF this year?" Artie asked Veronica.

"Yes, will you be speaking too?" she got her hopes up, desperate to not be alone in her nerves.

"No, but I'll be there," he mused, "Now I'm looking forward to it - to seeing your presentation."

"It's not like it's a symposium like William's, it's really no big deal," Veronica tried to downplay the attention now, imposter syndrome creeping up.

"Sure, it is. You've got so much to share about the botany collection," Jane assured her. Veronica thanked her, and from there Jane called it a night and said her goodbyes.

It was coming up on the end of staff happy hour, and Veronica sensed herself not wanting time with Artie to end.

"I've got to head out," she told him. She wasn't sure where it came from: maybe it was the fact that he boldly came up to her earlier like they were old friends, or maybe it was the second beer she had just finished, but she continued, "Before I go, do you want to see a part of the museum that many people never get to see?"

He smiled, almost wicked, his slightly longer dark hair was a riot of waves that fell into his face as he nodded, and quickly blurted, "Absolutely."

Dropping her empty drink into the recycling bin as she walked out the door of Classroom B, Veronica heard Artie's empty drink clink in the bin on top of hers. He followed her down the hallway, past other classroom doors and closed offices, zigzagging through the dim staff-only halls. It was technically after-hours, and the hallway lights were set to turn on with a motion-sensor, and only every other bulb illuminated. The effect was almost liminal, the path in front of them only lighting as they pressed forward.

Along the way she gave him an overview tour, pointing to various offices as they came into view, storage rooms, and even the library, until they ended up in the bird division.

She paused at the entrance to the bird prep lab, where they prepared bird specimens as study skins. He stopped next to her, leaning on the doorframe, looking at the cabinets and counters in front of them.

"Birds?" he prodded, almost unimpressed. For a moment she questioned if this was a good idea. She remembered how she thought he was like Henry, but shoved the thought aside and told herself he's shown her that he's not. He showed up to the pop-up event without needing to. She decided to believe that he cares about sharing science, and she wanted to share this with him.

"Not birds," she leered, leaning closer to him, fearlessly, "Bugs." The alliteration ricocheted off her lips, and he stared at her mouth since she was suddenly so close.

Veronica walked to the other side of the lab, to the first of two large, sealed gray doors. Expecting him to have followed her, she turned back to see he was still leaning on the doorframe at the entrance of the bird division. She waved him over. "William showed this to me, and he explicitly told me then that there is only one rule. The rule is that I can't open the second door without closing this one first," she pointed to the gray door before her.

That seemed to entice him, and he bounced off the door frame and slid right behind her. She opened the heavy gray door to let them both in. Once inside the small vestibule, just big enough for four people, she closed the first door, sealing in silence with them. In the close quarters of this quarantine room, she could feel his body heat as she eased past him to get to the second door. As soon as she opened it, they could both smell what lay ahead, and she quickly walked in. He didn't move at first, but she instinctively reached back toward him in the vestibule, grabbed his hand in hers, and pulled him in with her, closing the second door shut tight.

After Veronica confirmed that door number two was indeed securely closed, she turned around to face the room, but found Artie standing right in front of her, his chest blocking her view. His head was bent down, he was that close, holding eye contact intensely.

"What... is that smell?" he said, coldly, and it reminded her of the way Henry brushed off her suggestion for volunteers in anthropology, like it was the stupidest idea in the world. For a moment she felt insignificant, and like maybe this wasn't as impressive as she thought.

"Scavenger beetles," she replied, unsure of herself. She took a beat before gaining her confidence back, realizing this was a chance to educate someone about museum work that she found important, and fascinating. Veronica continued, standing taller, "Actually, the scent isn't the beetles themselves, it's the bird carcasses. The dermestid beetle colony is feeding on the decaying flesh. They are having dinner while simultaneously doing the scientists in the bird division a favor by cleaning the bones better than any bird preparator could."

He looked at her blankly at first, and then stepped back and took in the sight around him. The room was barely larger than a broom closet, with counters all around the perimeter. On each counter, multiple large, glass pet enclosures housed hundreds of beetles, rhythmically munching on what remained of bird skeletons in trays. With the silence between them, the only thing that could be heard was the gentle crinkling sound of the beetles eating.

Artie walked over to peek into one of the enclosures, getting a better view of the beetles and the bones. He turned toward Veronica and gave her a smile that said he was fascinated, too.

Feeling confident again, she shared what she knew from other museum staff, "The bird division is constantly getting migratory bird specimens, and these beetles are essentially museum staff too, doing their job to prepare the bird specimens for our collections."

"That's amazing. Smelly, but amazing," Artie expressed, moving from one glass enclosure to another to see the different stages of bird skeletons, from super clean and white bones to meaty and dark red and brown, almost black tissues.

"The bird specimens can tell us a lot about bird migration, and their biology in general. Across the city, birds that died in the migration used to just be tossed, never to be studied. But by partnering with different communities and commercial buildings, our bird division can capture a portion of these birds, and by using them for science, we can at least ensure that their lives weren't wasted," she went on, staring at the little beetles, all of them working on a Friday evening.

Artie looked at her, and she sensed his gaze. Veronica returned the stare when he speculated, "Does everything have to have a purpose or last forever? Can't some things just be special because they temporarily existed, just to exist?"

Veronica paused, not expecting to have such a thoughtful and interesting take from him. Perhaps he was starting to catch on to the fact that not wasting life was somewhat of a sensitive spot for her. She considered it, and nodded a little, agreeing in a way, but not fully committed to the idea.

On their way out, she told Artie, "The double entry doors are a protection to ensure that the dermestid beetles never find their way out. While they are useful to the bird division, if they found their way into the other collections, they could consume irreplaceable specimens and artifacts."

"Henry would be furious if one of these were found in the anthropology collections."

"Exactly."

Once they were safely on the other side of the double gray doors, Artie stared off into the distance and shared, "I'm not sure if I wanted to ever know what that smelled like."

"Yeah, I always feel like I need a shower after I spend time in there," she replied innocently, but then as she caught his eyes, she sensed a pause, brief, but there.

His Adam's apple bobbed, and - did she imagine it? Did he look down and pause at her lips, before looking down at his feet?

Desperate to lighten the mood, Veronica continued, "But think of the stories you'll get to tell all your friends about the flesh-eating beetles in the museum you're working in!" She flashed a big grin that was contagious.

He smiled back, which then turned into a laugh while he nodded approvingly. His smile looked just as good under the bright lab lights as it did in the hazy glow of Classroom B.

"Memorable, for sure," he uttered. He put his hand through his hair, and she couldn't tell if it was because he was feeling nervous and unsure of what to say next or trying to kill time while he thought of a way to end the evening. She still couldn't read him, but she found herself with the urge to follow his hands and put hers through his hair too.

"I should head home," she offered.

"Yeah, I'll do the same. Thanks for the thrill," he said, and gave a soft tap on her arm affectionately.

They parted ways at the entrance of the museum. Artie headed to the parking garage, and Veronica headed the opposite direction, taking the pedestrian pathway through the park and to the closest train station.

When she arrived at the entrance to her apartment, the downstairs neighbor's dog welcomed her home with a bark through the window. She unlocked her door and climbed the steps to her home. Typically, she would start on making dinner when she got home, but she headed straight to her shower first.

The scent of the dermestid beetle colony may not have physically lingered on her, but mentally she wanted to wash off. That, and her mind kept focusing on how close Artie stood to her, and the spot he touched on her arm. She wanted to wash off so that she would cool off from the thoughts of touching him again.

Chapter 9

Veronica spent some of her free time that weekend preparing for the conference. She knew William wouldn't mind if she put in hours during the workday on her presentation, but she felt that she was already behind. Her motto for putting in extra work outside of her traditional work hours was only if the extra work would make her feel better, and only if she would *not* end up resenting having to work the additional time. In this case, it would make her feel better to put some time in.

She outlined her presentation and her slides. Veronica figured she would get a rough draft of her ideas down on paper, and on the slide deck, and would come back later to refine it and make the design more professional.

After feeling like she made some progress on the bare bones of the presentation, Veronica began to practice out loud to get a sense of how long her presentation was with what she had thus far. She had 10 minutes to present, and an additional 2 minutes for questions.

She wanted to memorize most of it to ease her nerves, but she also wanted to come off naturally, conversationally. She ran through it a few times on her own, and felt confident practicing to just herself, in her own apartment, surrounded by the comfort of her plants and her home.

She remembered what William had suggested – that she needed to practice in front of someone. That made sense that she'd have to up the stakes, increase her nerves a little bit since she would eventually have to present in front of actual people. Some of the conference attendees will be people she knows from the museum, or even from her biology courses at university through the years. Others will be complete strangers.

She texted someone she could always count on.

VERONICA: *Are you free? I need your ears*

CAMILLA: *I'm always here to listen. What's got you down?*

VERONICA: *No, nothing like that! I need to practice my presentation for the conference. Can I practice in front of you?*

CAMILLA: *As much as I would rather listen to some gossip, I'm all yours. Come over.*

In a matter of minutes, Veronica tossed her laptop into a tote bag and grabbed her coat and keys. A short train ride later, and she found herself in Camilla's living room.

Camilla lived in the neighborhood next to Veronica's, just two train stops closer to downtown. Her apartment was the garden unit below a couple of people who were night owls. And while Camilla loved to go out at night herself, she found that her sleep schedule was the opposite of those living above her. At night, when she would be trying to sleep, they would be up and inadvertently making noise as they moved about the apartment. Once Camilla's lease was up, she knew she wanted to move to another apartment.

"I'm so glad you aren't moving far. I've been spoiled with such a short train ride to visit you," Veronica sighed, as she got herself comfortable on her friend's couch.

"I think I'll be the same distance away, just in the other direction," Camilla smiled at her friend.

"Good, I don't know if I'd ever see you again if it was any farther," Veronia teased.

"Try dating outside of your neighborhood. I swear, it's impossible. It feels like you have nothing in common with them!" joked Camilla.

Veronica tensed at the suggestion of dating. It had been years, and yet she continued to tell herself that she wasn't ready yet. She moved on to the reason for her visit, "I've practiced the presentation on my own a few times already, but it's different with an audience."

"How much time do you have to speak?"

"Only ten minutes. Which feels equally short and long at the same time."

"Let's see what you've got."

Veronica stood from her comfortable place on the couch, and practiced in front of Camilla. As nervous as she was to say her presentation in front of someone for the first time, she felt like the pressure wasn't so high. For one, it was her best friend Camilla, and second, her friend wasn't even in the industry. She knew her friend wouldn't be scrutinizing little details, but would also be there to share feedback honestly on Veronica's public speaking skills so far.

"How did I do?" Veronica asked when she was done.

"You're perfect, you don't need to change a thing!"

"You really mean it? Or are you just being a support friend?"

"I'm being honest. I think you paced it really well. As someone who doesn't know much about museum collections, just a little from you, I found it interesting but also a little nuanced. I learned something! That's the point, right?"

"Right. Thanks, Camilla," Veronica said to her best friend, before adding, "But maybe I need to practice in front of someone that actually makes me feel nervous, like my boss. That would re-create the moment the most accurately." Veronica let out a sigh.

"You'll be all nervous but at the end of the day, I know you're going to feel so good about your presentation!" Camilla's enthusiasm was always at a level 10, and Veronica was grateful for that at a time like this. She took a deep breath to calm her nerves about the presentation, but found that her nerves were still there. And thinking about people that actually make her feel nervous, there was one person that kept coming to her mind recently.

"Remember the postdoc fellow I mentioned?" Veronica asked, trying to keep her tone casual as she returned to the couch with her friend.

"The anthropologist?" Camilla replied, fiddling with the hem of her sweater mindlessly.

"I don't know if it was the fact that we were in a tight space together, or what... but I definitely can't stop thinking about him."

Camilla stopped fiddling, "Oh? I need more info! What tight space?" Veronica could always count on Camilla to be the most animated. Camilla practically crawled her way on the couch closer to Veronica.

"We had a nice chat at happy hour, and it led to me showing him the dermestid beetle colony."

"Right, right, right, natural location for a lover's tryst," Camilla deadpanned.

Veronica tossed the closest throw pillow in Camilla's direction and moaned, "Listen, I don't know how to feel about this, so I don't know if I can handle any teasing."

"Alright, alright, I concede. I want to hear what happened next. I'm listening."

Veronica paused, thinking to herself, and then replied, "Well, nothing really happened. We talked about science, he let me gush, he seemed like he was really listening, and all I know is that I want to spend more time with him."

"Simple as that, huh?"

"Simple as that."

Camilla stared at Veronica, which made her wonder what was going through her friend's mind.

"What? What are you thinking?" Veronica asked Camilla, making her brows meet in the middle.

"Well, like you said, nothing really happened. If it was me, something would have happened," Camilla replied absentmindedly, picking lint off her sweater before putting 'happened' in air quotes.

"Camilla! We were at work!"

"Yes, but not *working*."

Veronica shook her head. She couldn't quite process what it would mean to make a move on someone else that worked at the museum. Let alone within the perimeter of her workplace.

"Camilla, I couldn't. Could you?"

"We have *very* different workplaces," Camilla stated as a matter of fact. Marketing agencies weren't known for warm and fuzzy work environments. It was cutthroat, long hours, and yes, Camilla had seen coworkers get a little too friendly before.

Veronica buried her face into the couch cushion.

"Hey now," Camilla urged, "I'm not saying that I would, and I'm not saying that you should. What I want to help you figure out is *if* you want to, and how you're going to get there."

Veronica emerged from the couch cushion, her nose pink from pressing against the fabric, and hair tousled and frizzy around her face. Her friend was really good at helping her work through things, and yet at times, Camilla's strong-willed personality didn't know when to back down.

"You know my confidence isn't what it used to be in that department. Not since Noah," Veronica faltered, her voice succinct wanting to leave the conversation at that.

Camilla nodded at the name of her best friend's long term ex-boyfriend. "I know, but don't beat yourself up over it. We all have insecurities from the past. I know he left you for someone else - but not everyone will do that. Anyone might be capable of that, but that doesn't mean you should avoid pursuing something with them." Knowing how much Veronica struggled to get through that breakup, Camilla put a hand on her friend's arm.

"I think I'd like to talk about something, or someone, else now," Veronica looked sullen. Her friend complied, dropping the subject.

"Want to watch some bad reality TV?" her friend offered.

"By bad, you must mean good. And yes. But nothing focused on couples - please."

"Does that mean no to Vanderpump Rules?" Camilla asked with a disappointed look.

"I meant no Bachelor universe shows," Veronica grabbed the remote and pulled up the show that Camilla requested.

While Veronica was able to concentrate on the comfort of rewatching an old season of Vanderpump Rules, part of her mind drifted to standing close to Artie in the entrance to the room with the dermestid beetle colony. And with that, she had a small hope that it wouldn't be the only time they found themselves in close quarters. And like a wish, it would come true.

The next week at work, another flower showed up in her interoffice mailbox. This time, it was a daisy. More specifically, a *Bellis perennis* specimen. But that was as specific as it got. Like the last specimen that appeared mysteriously in her mailbox, many of the details that were typically on a herbarium label were left off.

Veronica remembered that she had planned to talk to the volunteers to find out where these came from. With the daisy specimen still in her hands, she looked around her desk for the violet she had shown to William. She found it in a corner, partially under some other papers.

It had been about a week since she received the violet, but she couldn't remember exactly when it arrived. But now, as she brought both specimens together, one thing she noticed was that they were recently collected, not as dry or aged as the museum collections. The green stems were more saturated in color than the usual dusty sage she was used to seeing in the museum's collections. Some of the herbarium specimens she regularly worked with were collected right there in the Midwest in the late 1800's, so of course their color and their fragility was much different than the more recent specimens before her.

Veronica left her office and brought the two flower specimens to the museum's herbarium. The collections room was quiet, as well as the small reading room where they kept old field expedition journals that needed to be transcribed. Looking for someone in particular, Veronica kept searching.

She made her way to the digitization room, which was barely larger than a closet. Inside she found exactly who she was looking for, taking photos of botanical specimens that were going to be added to the database.

"Pilar, just the person I wanted to see," Veronica said. "Do you have a second?"

Pilar looked up from the digital camera that hovered above the plant specimen below it. Her light hair was cropped just below her chin and flew in many different directions. She had tiny, earbud headphones in her ears, which she pulled out when Veronica entered the room.

Pilar was the longest volunteer that Veronica had, and all the other volunteers trained under her. Pilar sat back from the camera setup and said, "Shoot."

"Are these a part of the collection? Did any of the volunteers find some specimens without much label information?" Veronica inquired. She held out the two flowers that were neatly pressed on paper. Pilar took them in her hands to get a closer look.

"I haven't seen them, and no one's mentioned them to me," Pilar handed the specimens back to Veronica. "Were they found in the collections room?"

"That's the thing, they ended up in my office mailbox. But there were no notes, and no one has mentioned them. Not even William recognized them, and he's been here for ages." Veronica looked down at the mysterious flowers in her hand. "Though they look more recently collected..."

"Yeah, those puppies look pretty fresh compared to these specimens I have here that were collected in 1899," Pilar motioned to the specimen under her camera lens, and the stack of specimens next to it, waiting to be photographed.

"1899, really?" Veronica leaned over Pilar's desk to get a closer look.

"Yeah, collected right here in the Midwest, over a hundred years ago."

Veronica appreciated moments like this in the botany collection. Over a century ago, this plant lived, the world a different place, an entirely different generation of people living and breathing.

"Sorry I couldn't help you. But I'll ask the others when I see them. See if someone forgot to include a note," Pilar said, reaching for her earbuds.

"Don't sweat it, I'll ask around too. I'll let you get back to it, thanks though." Veronica waved goodbye and left the room as Pilar put her headphones back in and went back to digitizing the stack of specimens on the table.

Veronica made her way back to her office, the flowers still a mystery. She figured she would ask the newer volunteers about the specimens next time they were in. But she had a feeling that if Pilar didn't know about them, that they wouldn't either.

She stacked the specimens in the corner of her desk again, out of sight. She needed to get a start on her work week, and two specimens - in a museum of 40 million total - could wait.

Part Three

Jasmine

Chapter 10

Veronica sat at her desk and after reviewing her presentation slides repeatedly, the words started to all look the same. Veronica knew she had to switch tasks, move her body, do something, anything, different before she became absolutely useless for the day and burnt out.

Right as she was about to step away from her computer, she saw an alert pop up about a new email, the museum's weekly e-newsletter. A mindless read, Veronica decided she would read it as a palette cleanser. She read through press highlights of the *T. rex* fossil moving from the main hall to its own exhibit hall, and skimmed through a section about the native gardens being planted on the museum campus the upcoming spring. And there, at the end, a quick blurb and a headshot of Artie was included.

Visiting Scientist Fellowship Awarded

The museum has selected a postdoctoral researcher, Arturo Ribeiro, to be awarded the Visiting Scientist Fellowship. Arturo started his fellowship this month, and will be working on preservation methods of anthropological collection objects and artifacts, under department sponsor Henry Anderson, Collections Manager of Anthropology. The fellowship is awarded to early career professionals and researchers who can use the museum collections to advance science, and their careers.

Veronica felt warm and fuzzy while reading the memo and stared at the headshot included in the email. It was Artie smiling, standing next to totem poles, likely in the Pacific Northwest. Veronica sat for a moment, letting her feelings wash over her.

Feeling like she still needed to get her body moving after staring at her conference presentation for so long, Veronica stood up from her desk and found her legs walking to the Anthropology collections.

She took the staff elevator down a few floors to the basement, where there was enough space to house a collection with large items like Anthropology. Veronica's staff badge didn't have access to the Anthropological collections, only scientists actively working on the collection had access to the area. She came upon the collections entrance door, and knocked, peeking through the window in the door for any nearby colleagues that might recognize her.

She was let in by a staff member she recognized from hallways and staff meetings, and casually mentioned she was looking for Artie, and they pointed her in his direction.

Veronica walked over to Artie's desk, and when he looked up from his computer, surprised to see her, he smiled, which Veronica took as a good sign that it was a pleasant surprise. His face showcased dimples that appeared like sparkles, shining when he smiled.

They exchanged quiet, "Hey's" as she got closer, standing across from him, his workspace separating them.

"I saw your photo in the museum e-newsletter," she gushed.

"Oh, yeah," Artie stammered, almost blushing and putting his hand on the back of his neck. "I had to submit a photo for that."

"It was great. Where was it taken?" Veronica urged him on.

"Vancouver," was all Artie replied. Was he going to be stand-offish and quiet? Veronica thought they were past that. She breathed a moment, figuring she would take the hint and be on her way if that was the case. Until after a long pause he continued, "I visited the summer after undergrad. It was the trip that inspired my graduate work focusing on preservation."

"That's pretty cool," she replied, picking up on his own inspiration and wanting to know more. "What was it about that trip that did it for you?"

"The totem poles. These massive, carved pieces of art that are so meaningful, yet have to withstand extreme weather and wood rot. I wanted to work up close with them. Knowing their existence is fleeting. I wanted to be right there, to see them, to feel them, knowing that one day something that beautiful could be gone. They can't last forever, so I wanted to learn how to preserve artifacts like them," he shared.

Veronica nodded, listening. *Tourist turned scientist*, she thought while eyeing him, eating it up.

Artie got comfortable enough in his own spotlight to shine it back on her, "What about you? What inspired you to study botany? To work with a museum collection?"

"Well, conservation, I suppose. I've always had an aversion to waste. Flowers are cut every day to make floral arrangements for events, gatherings, weddings, funerals, just to be tossed when the day is over. Forests are cut back for commerce and capitalism." Veronica paused there, but Artie's eyes were still intently on her, so she continued, "I feel as though, if only we can just make sure that some plants aren't wasted. If we can study plant specimens, learn from natural history collections, and share with other scientists, maybe these cuttings aren't wasted."

They simply looked at each other, nodding in silent understanding.

"And digitizing the botany collections to share - it all makes sense," he nodded, assuring her that he recognized her work.

"I'm really a taxonomist, my specialty is neotropical taxonomy. The tropics tend to need the most conservation efforts." Not wanting to leave to go back to her own desk just yet, Veronica motioned to the work around him. "So, *visiting fellow*, show me what you've been working on."

Artie looked around his workspace, not sure where to start. He stood and walked a few feet over to the shelves of artifacts along the wall and his eyes scanned the items nearby. He reached up for an object and his shirt lifted, revealing the spot where his hip met his stomach, and the valley, the peaks, the deep caramel color. Veronica suddenly felt like she wasn't present; all she could think about was what was under his shirt.

He selected a box with a colorful mask resting inside. Bringing it over, he motioned for Veronica to come to his side to get a closer look. She hoped he couldn't sense her thoughts that were still on his torso, or the heat radiating off her body as she thought about it. Even under his shirt, his skin was the color of caramel, despite the Midwest winter months they were just emerging from.

He kept the artifact in its box, careful to not touch it directly since he wasn't wearing gloves. He pointed to the object, the tendons in the back of his hands peeking in waves, mesmerizing her. "This is a Haida mask from the collection. It's usually on display in the exhibition hall, but it's been removed for routine inventory and a preservation check. The blue paint in particular is more susceptible than other colors to the light in the halls. We do our best to have the lights low, and each display case is temperature and humidity controlled and monitored with thermometers. But the building is old and the mask even older. I'm comparing any wear on the artifact to past checks in our database, so that we can track deterioration."

"Are items ever removed from display permanently because of deterioration?" she asked, grateful to have something to focus on that wasn't his skin.

"For sure. There are some old textiles that would completely lose their integrity if left on display. The thinking is that they are best preserved in collections storage, available for specific research requests, rather than on display for all to see - especially if the general public is more often visiting to appreciate other, more well-known artifacts."

Veronica considered the conundrum of having artifacts that belonged to nobody, they belonged to the world. And yet, they were too fragile to be on display to share with the world, so in turn, they were shared with nobody. In that moment she had a great appreciation for Artie and the work he did, weighing the balance of sharing artifacts, but also caring for them to ensure they last many lifetimes. "You're really good at this, aren't you?" she gave a smile, hoping he felt the compliment.

"It's what I did my PhD thesis on, the effects of tourism on artifacts. And well, you *are* looking at the recipient of the museum's Visiting Scientist Fellowship after all," Artie joked as he leaned back, using sarcasm to hide any pride he felt from the compliment.

Veronica nudged his shoulder, teasing him for his response.

"Really though," Artie continued, "It's like the coral reefs. There are people who appreciate the beauty of the Great Barrier Reef, enough to want to visit and snorkel and see the ecosystem up close. However, if they really cared, they would realize that the worst possible thing for the reefs is to visit them. The damage that could be done within one, seemingly innocent snorkel visit takes lifetimes to undo." Artie was serious now, his tone morose and cynical. Knowing Henry, Veronica could see why they might get along. The realization made her want to wrap up their conversation, and not entertain getting to know him like she had been.

She nodded before saying, "Well, I'll let you get back to it. I should probably finish working on my presentation slides for the conference. It's coming up faster than I expected."

She started to walk away as she waved goodbye, and then she had a thread connect in her mind. Henry and her presentation. If Henry was going to be attending the conference like most leadership at the museum, maybe she could ensure he attended her presentation in support of his colleagues. Perhaps that could convince him to use her volunteer program and digitization efforts in anthropology.

Artie interrupted her thoughts and asked, "Will you be at happy hour this week?"

"Yes, I go most weeks with William," she replied, looking back at him. "Will I see you there, too?"

He nodded and said nothing else. His eyes fell to his feet, and he gave a soft wave.

Veronica left the anthropology collections area, and wondered if she imagined his face falling when they said goodbye, and if it meant he didn't really want the conversation to end, either.

Chapter 11

Happy Hour that week had Veronica and Artie falling easily into a routine of catching up with each other. At the end of Friday, Veronica wrapped up her work and left the Division of Botany before William. When she walked into Classroom B, Artie was already there and immediately said hello to her.

"How was your day?" he asked her, as they walked to get drinks.

"Overall, good. I had a loan request returned, so I re-inventoried it. Usually, we'll loan specimens for three months or so, depending on the research project. These neotropical specimens have been on loan for ten years, since before I worked here!" Veronica shared, incredulously. She grabbed a can of a local beer, dropped a few dollars into the communal bucket, and they walked to a corner of the classroom as she opened her can with a pop.

"Why did they need the specimens for that long?" Artie asked, sipping his own beer.

"They were supposed to return them ten years ago," Veronica laughed incredulously. "Better late than never? It was a loan that William had noted in a physical ledger before we started tracking loan requests on the computer. I still can't get over it - ten years! William had to track down the ledger in one of the old botany closets."

"An old botany closet, huh? What other hidden secrets of the museum are there?"

"You mean like how the housekeeping team refuses to clean the Ancient Egypt exhibition after dark? Those kinds of hidden secrets?"

Artie let out a breathy laugh, "Yeah, like that."

"It's the truth!" Veronica insisted. "I'm sorry to disappoint, nothing is as exciting as flesh-eating beetles as staff."

"Nothing fun?"

"Fun? Like juicy? There was one public event we hosted, and we caught some people making out on the fake bus in one of the exhibitions."

Artie laughed; his jaw fell a little in shock. And was that a hint of pink on his cheeks that she saw? "I meant anything fun that you're working on. In the botany collection?"

"You mean my collection of old, dried plants?" Veronica teased, on a roll.

He laughed again, and it sounded so good to her. She realized they were getting comfortable enough with each other that he was revealing more with her, and that she felt close enough that she could be a little silly with him. When he stopped laughing, he said, "Yes, Veronica, in your collection of old plants."

"Plants aren't as flashy as the anthropology collection, I assure you."

Artie gave her a deprecating look, "Don't minimize your work."

"Okay, okay," she thought for a moment. "William once helped solve a murder!" Veronica lifted her drink to take a sip while she let that sink in for Artie. He didn't seem impressed, so she went on, "A body was discovered with a particular species of moss growing on it. A species that was not local to the area where the body was found." She paused for effect, and continued, "William described what species the moss was and where it was typically found, helping the FBI confirm that the body had in fact been moved, and where it was moved from. Which eventually led to the conviction of the murderer."

"And some people think research is useless," Artie remarked, his voice flat. It was all he said. He didn't seem as impressed as Veronica, but she brushed it off, figuring she didn't tell the story as well as William did.

"But what about you - I want to hear what *you* are working on," he said.

"You know what I do. I digitize our botany collection," she responded, plainly.

"Is that so?" His voice raised at the end, almost like he was teasing her.

Veronica paused. It wasn't all that she did, and there was so much to come out of her digitization efforts all on its own.

"Well, recently some biologists have been able to use the historical records we've digitized to predict ecological trends in specific regions. Which is important in a world where our climate is changing rapidly. Climate change alone affects how plants and animals evolve, right? Botanists can study thousands of specimens through the years from our database, track them against climate patterns, and see how plants responded in warmer or colder years. Researchers use the geographical data on our specimen labels to track and monitor particular species that are invasive, and others that are endangered. There are even scientists that use AI to analyze our scanned specimens to quickly collect data points that would take humans *ages* to note manually." Once Veronica started, she could go on, but she paused, let herself inhale a big breath, and studied Artie's expressionless face. "I could talk about it for ages, unless someone stops me," she added finally.

"You make an impact, Veronica," he stated, his voice deep but unwavering.

"Yeah, but you personally and *physically* make a difference to the artifacts here. I'm just keeping an inventory of a collection and making it available to scientists," she replied, her first instinct was to not accept the compliment.

"Veronica," he replied, moving closer and wanting to stop her from deflecting a compliment, "The museum, and scientists everywhere, are lucky to have you."

When he put it like that, she blushed. And she loved hearing him say her name. It sounded so soft in his mouth, his slightest hint of an accent coming through with round vowels.

At that moment, William joined them in Classroom B, a drink in hand.

"Cheers to the last Happy Hour before the Association of Natural History Collections Forum," William said, raising his drink to the two of them.

"Too late to withdraw now," Veronica joked before taking a sip, shaking her head, hoping to shake her nerves away.

"You're going to do great," Artie reassured her, with a solemn face.

"A vote of confidence from one of the judges? You're all set, Sterling," William teased, calling Veronica playfully by her last name.

Veronica's eyes went wide, and she felt the blood drain from her face at the realization that Artie was one of the judges at the conference.

Sensing her realization, Artie clarified, "Judging the student competition."

Veronica's presentation wasn't in the student competition, and any sudden concerns about conflicts of interest faded away. *Did Artie sense the same concerns?* She wondered.

William left Veronica and Artie when another staff member pulled him aside to discuss the museum's upcoming summer internships.

"It's strange to think that summer will be here before we know it," Veronica said to Artie, her eyes drifting to watch William walk away.

"What are you looking forward to most in summer?" he asked her curiously.

"Biking around the city, biking through the state parks, even biking to work. What about you?" she responded, a faraway look in her eyes, lost in thought about her impending conference presentation, and the summer months soon after that.

"I don't really have plans this summer; postdocs don't tend to have much free time. Especially with adding this visiting scientist fellowship to this year, this happy hour each week is just about the only social thing I do."

"There's nothing else you make time for? You don't have just a few moments each week for your own hobbies?" she asked, astonished, and somewhat sad. "Having something just for me, like biking through the different neighborhoods, fills my cup, when so many things drain it."

"I mean, I play soccer with some friends, and I write," Artie offered.

"Yeah, I imagined all postdoc fellows spend a great deal of time writing," she taunted him.

"Yes, well, there's that. And there's also poetry," he shared, nonchalantly.

"Poetry?"

"Is that so hard to believe?" he took a sip of his drink while holding her eye contact the whole time.

"It's s-surprising," she stuttered, still unsure what to say about poetry.

"It's a creative outlet. When everything feels so clinical, something creative helps," he said pragmatically.

"Do you ever share your poetry?" Veronica let herself become curious about something in which she knew nothing.

"What, like poetry readings at cafes?" Artie joked, "No, I don't share."

"Do you ever let anyone read your poetry?" she insisted, not letting up.

"No one's ever asked to."

"I'll ask. Can I read your poetry?" Veronica inadvertently stepped a little closer when she questioned him.

For Artie, his poetry was just for him, a small escape. Having someone read his quick streams of consciousness felt invasive and he wasn't sure he was ready to be vulnerable enough to share.

"Someday," was all Artie replied.

"'Someday' sounds an awful lot like what people say when they really mean *never*," she quipped.

Glad to not have her push it, Artie returned the grin that Veronica gave him.

Without another word, he tucked a loose wave of her hair behind her ear. And it probably wasn't noticeable to the rest of the staff in Classroom B, but his finger trailed along her jaw for an inch or so as his hand made its way back to his side. Veronica felt it, and the nerves in her skin felt like they had just woken up from a decade long slumber. The hairs on the back of her neck stood like tiny soldiers.

"I like your hair," was all he said, and then they both sipped their drinks, giving their mouths something to do other than attempt to follow up to that statement. Veronica wanted to know the warmth of his hand near her face again. She wanted to know how well his hands would fit over her hips and cup her body. How his bare skin would feel up against hers.

Snapping her out of her unexpected thoughts, Artie asked, "My drink is empty, would you like one?"

Veronica considered it before deciding. "Actually, I'm going to call it a night," she proclaimed, and as much as she didn't want the moment to end, she needed to get home before sunset.

"I'll head out too," he replied, his voice quiet suddenly.

Veronica backtracked, not wanting to lose the feeling she just had, and added, "Not that I wasn't enjoying our chat. I just have an early train tomorrow morning, to visit my parents."

Artie nodded, "If you're taking the train tonight, I can drive you to the station."

She warmed to the idea of a perfect solution. A drop-off at the station would save some time, getting her home sooner. But also, she wouldn't have to say goodbye to him just yet.

"You don't mind? The closest train stop is the one I walk to."

"I definitely don't mind," he said, and then motioned to the doorway to exit.

"I have to grab my bag from my office, meet at the staff exit?"

Moments later, bundled in her coat and her bag in hand, Veronica walked through the doors of the staff exit and could see Artie waiting for her just ahead, the streetlights casting a glow around him. He smiled as she approached, and silently tilted his head toward the parking garage, beckoning her to follow.

Veronica couldn't help but glance around quickly, to gauge if any other museum staff were leaving at the same time and might grow curious as to why they were leaving together. She mentally pushed her worrying thoughts aside, assuring herself that a friendly drop-off at the train station was innocent. And yet, the way his hand had dripped down her jaw earlier didn't feel so innocent.

In the garage, the dim overhead lights led their way to the few remaining cars. Veronica followed Artie, each of them not speaking, and she was glad that there wasn't pressure to fill each moment with words just to end the silence. They both felt comfortable in the quiet between them.

"This is me," he said, pointing his keys toward a black car, unlocking the doors. They approached the passenger side, so he opened the door for her, and she slowly brushed past him, sliding into her seat.

Once he was in the car too, he handed his phone to her and let her pick the music. As he drove to the parking garage exit, she scrolled through his playlists, but her mind had trouble focusing on anything but the weight of him trusting her with his phone.

"'Music for micro-organisms'? Did you come up with this playlist?" she questioned as she hit play.

He laughed, "Yes, give it a listen, you'll understand why."

They listened to the lo-fi electronic music when a telling *ding* came through the car speakers. His phone vibrated in her hand, and she instinctively looked down at it.

Feeling like she was being nosy, she apologized, "Sorry. You got a text. From May," she read his screen, her best attempt at pronouncing the name that she had never seen before, *Mãe*. She dropped the phone into the console between them, feeling like she was violating his privacy by seeing a text of his from someone else. Someone else named Mãe.

"Mãe," he pronounced, his voice going deep with an accent. "My mom. Mom in Portuguese. I'm visiting my parents this weekend, too. She's probably asking if there's something specific I want to eat for dinner," he clarified as he glanced at her sideways.

"Oh," Veronica managed, swallowing her own insecurity after feeling a small bit of jealousy when she saw what she thought was another woman's name. "And what will you say?"

"I've been meaning to get back to her. I've been busy with the fellowship and actively trying to find a full-time position for after the fellowship is over."

It was the first time that Veronica heard him talk about life after the fellowship, life after the museum. Of course, his fellowship had a time limit on it, and some day he wouldn't be working at the museum, he wouldn't be going to the museum Happy Hours in Classroom B. If he was already looking into full time positions, maybe his fellowship was shorter than she expected.

"Everything she cooks is great," he stated, after Veronica's silence, looking over at her with a kind expression. "Her cooking always reminds me of visiting our family in Brazil."

They approached the train station, and he started to slow the car to drop her off.

"I can get out real quick," Veronica offered, trying to not be a burden.

"No, I'll park," Artie said mindlessly, as he pulled the car closer to the curb.

She watched him parallel park, his one hand on the wheel, and the other hand gripped the back of her seat's headrest. When he reached back, she caught a whiff of him, smelling warm, cozy, earthy, like insects trapped in amber, and a little clean like sudsing soap. His face eagerly looked back while parking, his chest opening up to her. It felt like time stopped. He caught Veronica staring, and he smiled. She quickly looked away, but a warmth found its way from the feeling of wanting to touch him to the embarrassment of being caught.

He surprised her by throwing the car in park quicker than she could protest. Just as fast, he was out of the car and met her on the passenger side, as she opened her own door. Artie grabbed the passenger door as she stood, somewhat blocking her way.

"I'll wait until you're on the platform," he declared, as the elevated train roared above them, racing toward Veronica's apartment.

"You don't have to do that, it might be a minute until the next train," Veronica insisted.

"It's no problem, really," Artie's expression was serious, and he stared at her. "I'll sleep better knowing you at least made it on the train platform safely, with other people around this time of evening."

Veronica appreciated the attentive words and thanked him. He stood so close to her, still blocking her way. Wanting any excuse to be close to him, she went in to hug him goodbye. Through their light spring coats, she wasn't sure if he felt the tension between them, but she memorized every curve she could make out through the fabric of his denim jacket.

"Let me give you my number. Will you text me when you're safely home?" he asked after the hug stopped.

"Sure. But I promise you, I take this train every day. I'll be alright."

"Let me have an excuse to give a beautiful woman my number," Artie insisted, holding eye contact with her. He smirked, and his dimples barely appeared.

She tried to stop her smile and to stop the pink blush that grew on her cheeks, but her face had a mind of its own. Her stomach swirled with nerves, but it felt so good to know he wanted her number.

"Sure," she said through her smile. Veronica took out her phone to enter his number as he announced it.

"Talk to you later," he beamed as a command, not a request, and he closed her passenger side door and watched her walk through the turnstiles, swiping her public transit card.

When Veronica got through the turnstiles and climbed up the stairs to the elevated train platform, she looked down at the street below. She could see Artie still standing exactly where she left him, though this time he was leaning on the hood of his car, looking up, expectantly.

Her train arrived and took her and spit her out a few blocks away from her apartment. The whole train ride was a blur, she was lost in her thoughts of the night, of the week, of Artie.

She climbed the stairs up to her apartment and thought of what to text him. She took off her shoes, plopped her bag down by the door, and fell into the couch with her phone in her hands. She typed.

VERONICA: *It's Veronica. I'm home, thank you for the ride*

ARTIE: *I'm home too, and thank you for your number*

Veronica didn't want their texts to end as quickly as they started, but she could only think to add one thing.

VERONICA: *Good night*

ARTIE: *Good night, Veronica*

ARTIE: *See you at the conference*

The conference was days away and would be the next time they saw each other. It would also be the first time that Veronica had to speak about her work in front of an audience. She suddenly felt anxious at the thought and rolled her face into her couch pillows to hide from the week ahead, wishing she could stop time to enjoy her night with Artie a little longer.

Veronica woke up early the next morning and quickly packed a weekend bag to visit her parents. She didn't have a car, so she booked a seat on the commuter train that would take her to the farthest end of the rail. In a car, it would be an hour's drive, but on the train, it was an easy two hours in which she typically found herself reading a book, or staring out the window watching the cornfields get taller the farther from the skyscrapers she went.

Veronica got her dark hair and her fastidious personality from her mom, Josephine, who worked in finance her whole life and always lived in the suburbs in quiet neighborhoods. Her mother tended to be the one to worry, and to generally be a rule-follower. Gardening was what her mother found meditative and calmed her nerves the best. Veronica took after her mother in that way, tending to worry rather than letting things roll off her back.

Veronica's younger sister, Melinda, on the other hand, took after their dad, Jerry, who had light hair, was an artist, and was more carefree and easygoing. Melinda's hair was golden like their dads, which was a stark contrast to Veronica's darkness.

When Melinda pulled up in her old Monte Carlo car to the train station to pick Veronica up, she had one hand in a box of spicy Cheez-Its, the other on the wheel, and a bad attitude.

"Hi," was all Melinda said, her window rolled down to let the cool air in.

"It's nice to see you too," Veronica replied to her sister, plopping down in the passenger seat after she tossed her bag in the back. "What's mom making for dinner?"

"What she always makes when you visit," Melinda replied, a handful of Cheez-Its making their way into her mouth.

"Chicken pot pie," Veronica mumbled happily, her mouth watering at the idea of a comfort meal cooked by her mom.

They were only twelve months apart, so their parents celebrated their birthdays together every year. Growing up, people thought they were twins, they were so close in age, and they almost felt like it too. Even though she was barely a year younger, Melinda still lived at home with their parents. She had changed her major twice, and was finally finishing up her undergraduate degree to work in cybersecurity. As sisters, they always got along well enough, but of course had their fair share of typical sister bickering.

After she parked her car, Melinda let them both into the house they grew up in, and called out to their parents that she was back.

The house they grew up in was comfortable. It wasn't the most up-to-date house on the block, but it was not seemingly outdated, either. They weren't rich, and weren't poor, just able to afford necessities, and maybe one or two nice-to-have things. Veronica's childhood had been pretty unremarkable, safe, and somewhat insulated, compared to all the variations of class she was now exposed to in the city. In the distance, she could see a familiar vase of fresh flowers in the kitchen, just like her mother always had done.

Josephine immediately came into the living room to hug her oldest daughter, and Jerry was already sitting on the couch as Veronica made her way to him to give him a hug, too. The flowers changed with the seasons, marking time as it passed.

Veronica and Melinda set the table in the kitchen for dinner, easily falling back into their routine and division of responsibilities when they are both in the home. Over dinner, Veronica's parents asked her a hundred questions about the conference and her presentation.

"Now, what exactly is the presentation about?" Jerry asked, his eyes narrowing as if it would help him absorb the words better.

"My presentation is called 'Expanding access and usage of natural history collections through digitization,' which is essentially what my job focuses on," Veronica explained.

"It's okay if you don't know how to talk about it to your friends," Melinda laughed, sensing that their parents weren't exactly following.

"Just say it's about making museum collections available to scientists everywhere," Veronica proposed.

Her parents nodded and offered praise, regardless.

After dinner that night, Veronica and Melinda stayed up late to catch up, reclining on the living room couch, both of their feet propped up in front of them, with Great British Bake Off playing on the TV. Veronica wore her childhood slippers that were cozy mostly because the fuzzy interior was worn down, perfectly shaped to her toes. Melinda was wearing shorts with cartoon pizzas on them, and a bowl of kettle corn popcorn propped on her lap that they were sharing.

Veronica's eyes fell to the coffee table in front of them and the large book that sat there. Their mom, a creature of habit, has had the same coffee table book always out. It was a book about planting and maintaining native gardens in the Midwest.

Veronica leaned forward to flip through the familiar pages. She could see her mother's notes in the margins, and sentences that she had underlined about certain plants that were better for pollinators, plants that complement each other when together, and sustainable gardening.

As she turned the warn pages, she came upon the center, where a single stem of a purple prairie clover flower laid flat, pale, and fragile from being tucked into the book many years ago. It brought back a memory for her, of all the years their mom would cut the flowers in the garden, to help the plants regrow in the next season. Her mom would display the flowers, and before they would wilt, she would let Veronica press them into big coffee table books.

This must have been one of the flowers that Veronica pressed, forgotten in the page, only to be reminded all these years later of how much she used to love saving the flowers. Cutting flowers felt so wasteful to her, and yet, her mother enjoyed their beauty in their home, and Veronica loved giving flowers a second life, pressed between the pages, immortalized forever. She felt that her value for things not being wasted was planted right there in those stems.

Next to the coffee table book, Veronica's phone buzzed. She instinctively picked up her phone, and then smiled when she saw who the text was from.

ARTIE: *Are you going to the conference welcome reception?*

"Gross," a voice groaned next to her, interrupting her thoughts.

"What?" Veronica asked her sister.

"Your smile. Must be someone special," Melinda taunted, her eyes not even coming off the TV screen.

"I have no comment," Veronica replied to her sister, her mind already thinking about what to text back.

"Oh, come on, who is he? Or she?" her little sister interrupted her thoughts, now looking at her, popcorn endlessly being brought to her mouth.

Veronica didn't answer her, but instead busied herself with her phone.

VERONICA: *It's my first time going to the conference, so I assumed I should. Why? Does no one go to those things?*

ARTIE: *Oh no, they go. Free food and drinks, they definitely go.*

ARTIE: *I'm packing. Will set aside some -*

A pillow landed in Veronica's lap before she could finish reading the text.

"Rude," she said to her little sister, eyeing her.

"Who is it?" Melinda nearly shouted as she paused the show that was on the TV. That was how Veronica knew she wasn't kidding around.

Veronica considered how much she wanted to share at that moment. While nothing had explicitly happened between the two of them yet, Veronica felt like she was reading the signals right. Things had really changed since she had first met him. Now, he took many opportunities to be around her at the museum, to talk to her when they were in the same room, and he asked for her number. Veronica wanted all of those same things too. He had said he liked her hair and even called her beautiful. She felt the anxiety growing in her stomach, the nerves that came with the excitement of wanting to spend more time with someone. Because Veronica knew all too well the risks that came with getting close to another person.

She looked at her little sister, who was practically a twin, they were so close in age. "He is someone I met at work. But he isn't staff, he's a visiting scientist," Veronica finally replied, feeling like she had to defend that this was not an inappropriate working relationship.

"Is he a botanist too?" her sister asked.

"No, an anthropologist."

"Oh, like Indiana Jones," Melinda gushed.

Veronica laughed at her sister's endless supply of pop-culture references. "Indiana Jones was an archeologist, not an anthropologist," Veronica clarified, and yet she was now thinking of Artie in the classic Indiana Jones outfit, and what the rest of his tanned torso might look like with his shirt unbuttoned a bit.

"And the difference is?" her sister asked with a mouthful of popcorn.

"Indiana Jones focused on recovering remains and objects. Artie studies anthropology, which is more focused on the cultural components of human groups, past and present."

"Artie, huh?"

"Yes, his name is Artie. Arturo, but only his boss calls him that," Veronica recalled the only time she had heard his formal first name, when Henry introduced him.

"Arturo, nice. Better than Indiana. Anyway, I'm glad to hear that someone is making you smile like that, but can we get back to bread week?"

Veronica was happy to end the conversation there with her sister. They finished that episode of the show, and then called it a night. Veronica laid down in her bedroom, which had changed a bit since she used to live there. Unlike Melinda, Veronica went away for undergrad. During that time, many of her childhood posters and decorations had been boxed up and stored in the closet for Veronica to take someday. Though much of the furniture was the same, her parents had decorated the room to be more of a general guest bedroom.

She checked to make sure her door was closed, and then looked at her phone to finish reading the text she had started to read earlier.

ARTIE: *I'm packing. Will set aside some clothes for the reception too then*

Veronica finished reading the rest of his text. She made a mental list of outfits she'd also have to pack. *Outfit to present in, travel outfit (there and back), attending other sessions outfit, welcome reception outfit.* Her list was growing. She texted back.

VERONICA: *I'm glad I won't have to awkwardly network at the reception solo. It'll be like museum happy hour, except off-site*

ARTIE: *Yeah, just like happy hour*

Veronica wondered if any of Artie's conference outfits would include a button-up shirt, like Indiana Jones, and that's when she promptly decided she had thought enough about his wardrobe, and what his body might look like underneath.

Chapter 12

Veronica was back in the city, on the elevated train. But this time, she was on the train to the airport, her carry-on luggage in tow. She had packed for the conference when she got back from her parents house, and checked and rechecked her packing list multiple times.

She didn't regularly fly in an airplane, but when she did, she was a nervous flier. This time, she was more nervous than usual. Not only did she have her regular airplane nerves, but she had nerves thinking about her presentation ahead.

Veronica moved almost mindlessly through the airport, her brain on autopilot to get her all the way through landing in California. Once she arrived, she checked into her hotel where the conference was taking place. Veronica ditched her bags in her hotel room and decided to get the lay of the land before the conference started officially the next day.

Registration was the only thing already open, for the early arrivals like herself. She checked in with the registration team, and they gave her a badge with a gold label at the bottom that read "Presenter." Making sure it was real, she rubbed the smooth cardstock between her fingers, and then along the rough lanyard embroidered with the letters that repeated "ANHCF" like a chant. The registration team also gave her a tote bag filled with sponsor swag, and a program for the conference.

As soon as Veronica stepped out of the registration area, she immediately flipped through the program. She knew exactly what she was looking for.

There, on the program in her hands was her name, among many others, but her name nonetheless:

Presentation*: Expanding access and usage of natural history collections through digitization*
Presenting Author: **Veronica Sterling**, Botany Collections Assistant, Midwest Natural History Museum
Co-Author: William Sawyer, Head of Botanical Collections, Midwest Natural History Museum
Co-Author: Pilar Torres, Division of Botany, Midwest Natural History Museum

It felt so real to see it in print. The last thing to make her believe her eyes was to see the room she would be presenting in. She didn't want her first time seeing it to be moments before she had to present.

Veronica made her way down the hall, each corridor looking the same as the last in the vast conference center. She finally saw signs pointing to the room her session was assigned to.

Slowly approaching the door, she put her ear towards it first, listening for any sound of people inside setting up. She heard nothing, so she carefully pushed the heavy door open enough to peek.

Inside she saw the stage already set, with a screen off to the side, and a table for various audio-visual equipment. The room was full of chairs, all facing the stage. Veronica wasn't sure what she was expecting but was glad to see that it wasn't the largest room that she had ever seen, and it was not as small as she worried it would be, either.

She closed the door as quietly as possible as she exited, just in time for her phone in her pocket to vibrate. When she looked to see who was messaging her, and she saw a small image of her and Camilla, squeezing their heads together to fit into the small frame of the contact photo.

CAMILLA: *How's California? Wave hello to the Pacific Ocean for me (get it?)*

Veronica's nerves had eased, and she was able to breathe a sigh of relief now that she had seen the room, and a friendly message helped.

CAMILLA: *Don't forget, the newest version of your slides are titled "V3-Final (1)" - not just "V3-Final"!*

Veronica smiled knowing she could always count on her friend.

VERONICA: *What would I do without you? I'm heading to upload the slides now while it's fresh in my mind.*

Veronica looked at the program to find the room name of the upload room. Once inside, she found an empty laptop and rummaged through her bag until she found her favorite USB drive. It was in the shape of a cactus and was a souvenir she picked up from the gift shop of the botanical garden not far from the museum.

She found the file, "ANHCF-Sterling-Slides-V3-Final (1)" (not to be confused with "ANHCF-Sterling-Slides-V3-Final") and tapped through each slide to make sure everything lined up on the conference's system.

Veronica grabbed her trusty cactus-shaped USB drive and took a breath. Although it was one less thing she had to do, it was a step that made her that much closer to her presentation in the coming days, and her stomach dropped at the thought.

It was the first full day of the conference, so Veronica was up early to make a cup of coffee in her hotel room, grab a granola bar as a quick breakfast, and then off to the opening keynote session.

Although it was her first time attending the conference, she happily recognized some faces from undergraduate and graduate school biology classes. She ran into a few former classmates, some who were carrying their scientific posters in cases slung on their backs.

After the opening keynote, her morning consisted of roaming from session room to session room, watching the presentations that she added to her schedule, including a symposium on citizen science, and a workshop on inclusive communities.

When it was time to find something for lunch, Veronica checked in with William and they decided to meet up at a nearby deli before their afternoon tour.

William had handled Veronica's registration for the conference since the museum was paying for both of them to present. When it came down to the registration process, he had signed her up for a tour of the local aquarium since he would be attending the tour as well.

The tour guide led their ANHCF group through the first-floor sea creatures. William loved seeing the octopus, while Veronica gushed over the sea otters.

At the end of the tour, William and Veronica found themselves on the second floor in front of the jellyfish tank, the oval viewing window looking into the sea nettles dancing on the other side of the glass. Their guide ended the tour and said goodbye, and their group dispersed to explore individually.

"You know, we have the aquarium on the museum campus, and yet I never go," Veronica said, filling the silence that settled between them as other aquarium guests roamed around them. Her neck craned up to the vast, blue expanse contrasting against the slow, pink jellies.

"We used to go. Each of the heads of collections would get together to knowledge-share and have a working lunch in the aquarium's cafe. It allowed for a change of scenery, as well as a third-party, neutral ground of sorts, to allow each of the museum divisions to feel heard. But schedules get busy, people fall out of habits," William replied somewhat sadly.

"There are a few people from the museum at this conference, right?" Veronica asked.

"Yes, a handful of collection heads that aren't presenting, just attending."

"We should have a team dinner," she offered, now looking over at her boss instead of at the ballet dance of jellyfish.

"The opening reception is tonight; most will be busy attending that."

"There's always tomorrow, the last night of the conference."

"You think everyone will want to get together for a last-minute dinner?"

"If anyone can persuade museum staff to get together at the last minute, it would be the Mayor of Museum Happy Hour," Veronica flashed a wide smile at him.

William nodded and mirrored her smile back. "I'll arrange it. But make yourself available tomorrow night."

"You got it."

At the conference reception, the attendees gathered in a nondescript hotel ballroom that was made more interesting by various food stations highlighting the local food scene. Veronica's eyes immediately zeroed in on the dim sum station, as well as a seafood station since fresh seafood was hard to come by in the Midwest. She waited in line to take advantage of the coast's seafood menu items and made small talk with the scientists in line behind her.

Once she had a plate of food, Veronica scanned the seating area for familiar faces. She spotted William at a small, round table with people Veronica didn't recognize, but there was an open chair next to him.

Veronica took the seat after she said hi to William and confirmed that no one was sitting there. William introduced her to

James, the older gentleman on his other side, who was the head of collections at a university in the Midwest.

They chatted and ate for a few minutes when Veronica saw someone approach their table from the corner of her eye. When she turned away from the conversation to look, Artie met her eyes.

"How was your flight?" Artie asked Veronica. He crouched down to bring himself to her level. In that position, he was looking slightly up at her, his knees wide, elbows resting on his thighs. The position felt both intimate and confident at the same time.

"Good, I made it. Yours?" she replied.

"I made it, too. Looks like you need a drink. I'll get us some, what would you like?" Artie asked. His eyes locked on hers, holding eye contact. *He knew what he was doing, didn't he*, she thought.

"I'll take a glass of red wine - but I don't have any cash on me," Veronica started to request, but then remembered the cash bar.

"I've got it. Be back," he replied, and just as smoothly as he arrived, he left.

Veronica went back to joining the conversation William was having with James. After a few minutes, Artie re-appeared at Veronica's side with a glass of red wine, and a beer for himself.

He stayed standing as he handed it off to her, and she thanked him. Realizing Artie had joined them, William interjected.

"Ah, we have company," William started. "James, you know my Veronica. And this is Artie, he is a postdoc fellow in the Anthropology division at the museum. Artie, this is James, he oversees the entire collection at the university in the city."

"Pleased to meet you," James said, extending a hand.

"Pleasure," Artie replied as he shook James' hand. Veronica noticed that his introductions were usually short, succinct, like he couldn't be bothered with a full sentence. She was finished eating, so she stood to chat with him.

Veronica wasn't sure if she imagined it, but suddenly Artie seemed a bit rigid, standing farther away, compared to before when he crouched close to her intimately.

"You okay?" Veronica asked, trying to read him. And when he didn't answer she filled the silence, "Do you know James from when you were at the university?"

"No, I never actually met him. I'm good," he said, a weak attempt at reassuring her.

"How was judging the student competition?" Veronica sipped her glass of wine and attempted to make small talk.

"Good. It was pretty much the same judging rubric as last year, so it was straightforward. This year, there was a training on implicit bias for judges, which is a great addition. Also, volunteering as a judge gets me brownie points with the association. Some faculty at universities are heavily involved with the association, and Henry has been encouraging me to pursue a postdoc position within a university lab after the fellowship ends. He thinks I'd enjoy being in a university setting."

"Is that what you want?"

"I could see a future where I'm in a lab, yeah. It does feel like a good next step for me."

Veronica nodded, thinking of the universities in the city that might be hiring, but also thinking about all the ones across the nation that Artie might pursue, too. She pushed away the idea of him moving away, knowing that she was getting ahead of herself.

"Talking about the student competition?" a voice, James', from just behind them, interrupted.

"Yes, Artie is one of the judges for the student competition," Veronica replied to James.

"Some of my students were in the competition, giving talks today. I hope they were up to standard," James said with a snide smile.

"All of your students gave talks, no posters?" Artie asked James directly.

"Yes," was all James replied.

Artie shifted from one foot to the other, and took the opportunity to elaborate on his question, "We are finding that students want to present talks, and posters seem to be getting less popular. But they are important on their own and serve their own purpose within the scientific community."

"I can see that - but I know when I interact with students at my university, I encourage them to present a talk instead of a poster. A greater challenge," James explained proudly.

Artie didn't look away. He held James' gaze and replied, "That's part of the problem then, isn't it? It's our jobs as the leaders for the next generation to teach them about the importance of certain aspects of the industry. We have the ability to guide and influence the next generation, and if we're telling them to present a talk and not a poster, then of course they aren't going to see the value of a poster. And yet posters are valuable - being able to present data and information in a succinct way - that's a skill. If we aren't keeping skill-building of the next generation at the forefront of everything we do as leaders, if we aren't helping craft the next generation of great scientists, then we aren't really leaders, are we?"

James and a few of the others at the table that had decided to listen in were now quiet. Veronica had almost forgotten that William was at the table as well, until she saw him smiling down at his hands and nodding in agreement. Slowly, James' head started to nod in agreement, too.

Veronica looked back to Artie, his eye contact still holding strong with James. In that moment, she saw the fox, the cunning and confident leader of the pact, not afraid to speak up for something he believed in. And Veronica really liked what she saw and heard.

"What about you? Being that this is your first year at the conference, and you're speaking at it, are you nervous for your presentation?" Artie tipped his beer to his mouth, not breaking eye contact with Veronica the entire time.

After the back and forth between Artie and James, James politely made his excuses and left their table.

"Nervous, yes," Veronica replied miserably. "And it's scheduled for the last day of the conference. I wish it was the first day so that I could just get it over with."

"I get it. But you're going to do great," he reassured her. He tipped his bottle of beer back and drank the last sip. As he lowered it, he glanced at her through the bottom of the glass, saying, "Here's looking at you, kid."

She paused, registering the phrase. "Casablanca?"

"A classic."

"My sister is a bit of a pop-culture junkie, consuming all contemporary media. In contrast, I love old movies almost as much as I love old plants," Veronica explained as her mouth curled up.

Artie enjoyed looking at her smile so much he resisted the urge to capture her grin for his own pocket. "Me too."

Veronica wasn't sure if she should say what she wanted to say. But then she did, anyway. "I should have known. I saw you. At the old theater."

"Oh?"

"A Streetcar Named Desire. I was there with my friend, Camilla."

"Another great classic film," he said. After a sip of his drink, he added, "Why didn't you say hi?"

"You were with someone."

"My sister," he said, almost too quickly. And while she knew why, she didn't want to admit it, but she felt a bit of a relief to have an explanation of who was with him that night.

William approached the duo and commanded their attention, "The reception is ending soon, so a few of us from the museum are moving this party to a nearby bar. Will either of you be joining?"

Veronica and Artie instinctively looked to each other to gauge the other's response. She felt herself not wanting the night, nor the conversation, to end just yet, and found herself replying, "I'm in."

"Me, too," Artie chimed in almost immediately.

The group of museum staff trickled down the street to the nearest bar, a casual game room style pub. Veronica's colleagues dispersed themselves at various tables, and William corralled a group to play a round of tabletop shuffleboard. Veronica made her way to the bar to order drinks with Artie. After receiving their drinks, the conversation started as effortlessly as it had ended at the conference reception.

"Your post-undergraduate trip, what made you pick Vancouver?" Veronica asked, as they sat at the bar next to each other.

"I wanted to take a road trip through the United States and Canada."

"Wow, that is the quintessential American experience."

"I had never left the city, remember? It was more so my interest in anthropology, really. I've always liked learning about different cultures, places, and communities. It was probably because of my family and our own culture." He shared, looking at her sideways, judging to see if he should go on.

"Your family?" she questioned. He planted a seed, and she was eager to know more.

"My parents were born and raised in Brazil. I was born here. And truthfully, I don't feel like I'm from Brazil since I wasn't born there and didn't grow up there. And at the same time, I don't feel like I'm from here, even though I've never really left. The rich food culture and music of Brazil makes me feel like a *Brasilero*. But being born an American, with parents whose first language isn't English, I've always felt like I was seeking to learn about cultures all around, to find out where I belong, which box I tick..." he stared off while he shared vulnerably, waving his hands animatedly, making the divide between here and there visible before them.

Veronica thought of her own family story and history of gardens and plant life and how it led to her passion for botany. Hearing his story humanized him, and she was grateful that he felt comfortable enough to share. *He wasn't like Henry at all,* she thought. He was just looking for a place where he belongs. Doing his best to adapt to his environment.

"Your recent family history is so rich. My distant, distant, *distant* family comes from England - hence my last name, Sterling," Veronica shared, and after a beat, added, "That explains the fox."

"The fox?" he questioned, not following, his eyebrows coming closer together.

"When we were at the museum happy hour, you said the animal that you would be is a fox. Adaptable to their environment."

"Yeah, you're right," he said, the memory coming forward before adding, "It's not just the adaptability. Foxes are also curious and can be aggressive."

"Well, by nature, all scientists are curious. Or else they wouldn't be scientists, would they?" she poked.

"I agree," he said simply, taking a small sip of beer, pressing his lips closed when he was done.

She couldn't let it go, she liked, wanted, needed to know, "And aggressive?"

"Hm?" was all he said.

"I haven't seen you be aggressive. Curt, maybe. But not aggressive," she pressed.

He looked at her thoughtfully, really contemplating his words until he said, "You might see it eventually."

Veronica considered if that was a threat, and while she had a feeling that she didn't want to see that side of him, she figured it was just something she would see evenutally, taking his word for it.

"And you, I know you are a botanist. You are undeniably passionate about what you do. What else? What do you like to do in your free time?" Artie asked.

"Me?" Veronica thought about how she would describe herself. "I like to bike ride. It feels kind of like an activity you can do that is multi-faceted. It takes you from place A to place B, you move your body while doing it, you can see all these parts of the city that you may have never seen before. Besides that, I end up either spending my free time with my friend Camilla and watching bad TV, or visiting my family in the suburbs. Also watching bad TV."

Artie looked at her thoughtfully and huffed.

"What?" she asked, unsure what he was thinking.

"That's not the first time you've mentioned something and somewhat making the most of it."

"You mean biking?"

"Yeah, but like you've said with other things before, making the most of it, not letting something be wasted."

Veronica considered this and realized that he must really be paying attention to the things she said. And at the same time, she felt somewhat insecure that there was a common thread he noticed.

She thought back to all those times her mom clipped a flower from the garden she spent so much time nurturing. Afternoons of her mom kneeled over pots of soil and seeds flashed in her head. Weeks of her mother patiently waiting until a tiny, green bud surfaced from the wet soil. Months of her mother watering the flimsy stalks, turning the pots *just so*, to catch the best sun. All that patience, all that care, just for it to come to an end when her mother snipped the flowers right from their roots. That's why she pressed those flowers between papers once they started drooping in their vases. To not waste them. To not waste all that time and care. She felt herself wanting to get defensive, until she sighed and finally asked, "Is that so wrong?"

"No, not at all," he reassured her, and yet continued, "I just think that there's also an opportunity to appreciate things that are worthwhile for the sole fact that they exist. Nothing more."

"I'm not sure I follow."

"Have you ever treasured something that's beautiful for the sole fact that it's beautiful, even if it's meaningless? A shooting star? When the trees look like they're on fire in the fall? The way the sun makes everything glow when it sets?"

Veronica thought for a moment, and with her pause, Artie wasn't sure if she was following.

"Okay, I've got another example. One of my favorite poems is about a cockroach and a moth, having a conversation. The poem is theoretically written by the cockroach by jumping on the keys of a typewriter. It's called The Lesson of the Moth. The cockroach asks the moth why it gets so close to the light, when the light could kill it. The moth explains how beautiful the light is, and that it would rather experience beauty, even if just for a moment, even if it kills them, than to never experience beauty at all. More eloquently said, naturally," Artie shared, and then sat back. "Good things don't last forever, and it's best to enjoy them, all consuming."

"I'm learning so much, Artie Ribeiro. But that feels like a bit of a sad way to look at things," Veronica loved hearing his perspective, but felt like she couldn't relate to that feeling at all.

"I feel like it's a pretty realistic way to look at things and gives me the greatest appreciation for the beauty in this world, since it is fleeting."

"Time is cruel."

"It can be."

Veronica took the pause in their conversation to look around. She noticed that many of their museum colleagues had left the pub, only a few remained. The ones that remained were museum leadership, like William and Henry. Seeing William reminded her that tomorrow would be her presentation, the reason she was there, in that bar.

"Looking for someone?" Artie teased, catching her gazing toward the other museum staff in the bar.

"No. Rather, just seeing who is still here."

Artie quickly looked around to assess and saw that the rest of their colleagues were mostly crowded around the shuffleboard table. Veronica's gaze had landed on William, familiar and commendable.

"If you'd rather join the group, we can," Artie offered, motioning toward the group.

"Actually," she started, and he pulled his body back immediately as she shared, "I'm feeling so nervous, anxious, I'm not sure what else. My presentation is tomorrow. This is the first time I'll be speaking at a conference. I don't know what to expect. I -" Veronica felt herself rambling and her heart rate increasing in speed.

"Hey, hey, breathe. It's scary, I know. But you've got this. I'm not just saying that. But as someone who truly enjoys listening to you speak about what you do, I'm sure everyone else is going to walk away from your presentation with only positive things to say."

Hearing his encouragement to breathe, his kind words about listening to her talk about the museum, her breath eased. And although her nerves about the presentation didn't go away, the anxiety in her stomach made room for butterflies. The nice kind of butterflies.

She took a big breath, and nodded, finding comfort in the pep talk.

At that moment, William came up to them and put an encouraging hand on Veronica's shoulder.

"We're heading out, we'll see you at your presentation tomorrow, right, Sterling?" William asked.

"I'll be there," she replied, and they waved goodbye to the rest of the museum staff. She locked eyes with Henry and offered a soft wave goodbye. He nodded his head and waved politely back.

Veronica yawned, and she chalked it up to jet lag. She looked at the time, realizing it was already past midnight back in the Midwest.

"We can head back," Artie said, catching her cue. He waved the bartender down and asked for the check. Before Veronica could get her own wallet out of her purse, he said, "I'd like to get this."

"Thanks, but I still owe you from the drink at the reception, too."

But his hand was gently on hers, assuring her.

"Thank you, Artie," she said simply, putting her bag away.

He placed his credit card on the bar, and she glimpsed his wallet, his driver's license sticking out a little.

"Let me see that," she pleaded, a smile on her face as she reached for his ID.

Artie instinctively pulled his wallet and ID away from her, out of her reach, but that didn't stop her from reaching. He found himself enjoying her stretching across his torso, and then he reluctantly let her hands close on his wallet.

Veronica took out his ID and inspected it. In the tiny portrait on the card, his hair was cut shorter, cropped close to his head on the sides, where now his waves were long enough to fall in his face. His honey-colored eyes looked practically black in the flatness of the image. But his dimples were still visible, as well as his iconically strong jaw, even though the rest of his face looked young.

"What?" Artie asked.

Coyly, her eyes darted from the ID to his face and back, and she said, "Let me pick out everything that is wrong on your ID from the way it does no justice to your face to the way you still look good through the laminate. It's unfair."

He gave a small, silent smile, and there might even have been the slightest hint of pink that flushed across his cheeks. His reaction to the compliment warmed Veronica from the inside out. She handed the ID back to him, and he made a point to linger on her hands when he took it from her. But he couldn't think of anything to say, so he just held eye contact.

Their drinks were nearly empty, their bill was paid, and the next day was approaching. Veronica saw Artie open his mouth, and close it again, as if there was something he had been wondering, something he wanted to - no, *needed* to ask her.

Veronica waited, holding space for his silence, unsure of what to say to encourage him to just say what's on his mind. And then, as if the number of drinks he had was finally sufficient liquid courage, he spoke.

"Are you into William?" Artie stopped making eye contact when he asked, which was rare for him.

Veronica couldn't even hide her shock if she tried; her disbelief came out as "He's my boss. We work together!"

"It's not unheard of," Artie said quietly. His eyes focused on the perspiration on the side of his empty bottle, smoothing it away with his thumb. Veronica couldn't bring her eyes to look at him, but instead her eyes followed his stare to the bottle, the condensation slowly forming droplets heavy enough to fall down the glass. It felt like her own beads of sweat that collected on her forehead in this warm bar. The heat of an accusation like that made her nervous.

She firmly shook her head back and forth, "No. What gave you that idea?"

"You're always with him, or going on about him," he said sheepishly. This time, he looked at Veronica, as if the confirmation was what he needed to hear in order to face her. "And the *way* you go on about him."

"Artie, I assure you, it's 100% because I love that he loves the museum, the collection, and the mission. His passion is infectious. I'm definitely a fan of his and consider myself lucky to work for someone talented, knowledgeable, and passionate about their work. But that's the end of it. There are no inappropriate feelings there."

He nodded, pausing for a few beats before asking, "Would it be so inappropriate to have feelings for someone you work with?"

Surprised, she tried to ask thoughtfully, "Work with closely?"

"Not directly..." he said almost immediately, but his voice volume trailed off.

"Do they know?" Veronica egged on, wanting more, needing more, but worried she'd scare him off. She kept it vague, but hoped he would fill in the blanks that she was too shy to ask directly.

"I don't see how she couldn't know," he said, almost laughing, turning to look directly at her.

Her heart raced, and she worried that the heat on her cheeks was as visible as it was warm. Veronica wanted him to be talking about her. But how could he be, if he's insinuating that she would know if it was her? And she felt as uncertain as ever.

"I think... if two people aren't directly working together in a department or on a particular project..." she paused to gauge his expression. His eyes dropped to her lips, as if desperate for the words to leave her mouth. Finally, more confident that she was reading the situation right, and before she lost her nerve, she finished, "then those two people could pursue it."

She felt anxious as soon as the words came out, and just as quickly, Artie's warm hands rushed to either side of her face, gently cupping her jaw to guide her mouth closer to his. And when he touched her lips with his, they felt soft, but the pressure felt firm. He lingered just a few moments, enough for Veronica to cherish the feeling, but short enough to leave her wanting more. When his lips broke away from hers, his hands were still tenderly on her cheeks, and she brought her own hand on top of one of his, willing him to not let go.

They stared at each other; Artie, the master of eye contact. But the look on his face seemed unsure.

"Was that okay?" He asked, lowering his hands, Veronica's own hand coming down to her lap.

It was a great kiss in the sense that it left her wanting more, but she couldn't find the words to describe how she was feeling right then. Instinctually, she grabbed his shirt collar and brought him closer to her, planting a firm kiss on his mouth this time, desperate for more. *Yes*, she said with her breath gasping the air that he was breathing, *more than okay.* She clenched the cloth underneath her fingers, and it stretched across his body - she was reading his shoulders, his torso, and his muscles through the give of the fabric. Where his t-shirt usually hung on his fit frame like sap, this time it stretched across him like rubber as she pulled.

Veronica kissed him with an open mouth, eager to invite his tongue in - but stopped with the realization that they were in a public bar, and she let go of his shirt.

When she planted one last, closed peck on his bottom lip, she let out an affirmative and breathy, "Yes. It was the world's okayest kiss."

She bit her bottom lip, wishing she could bite his, and her lips turned up at the corners, waiting for him to catch on that she was teasing him. Artie's grin spread across his face, slow like a tree growing, getting the joke, and then he took a hold of her hand. Sweet, and tender, he kissed her knuckles, as if he too was suddenly feeling shy amid a bar full of strangers.

"I meant, was it okay that I kissed you? I don't want to make you uncomfortable, or to complicate things. I'll still be conducting research at the museum for a few more months," he clarified.

Her own insecurities came rushing out as quickly as the heat in her cheeks did, "Do you regret it?"

He rolled his jaw, "You have no idea how little I regret it, and how much I want to continue."

Veronica blushed. "Should we leave?" was all she could think to say, feeling self-conscious for practically making out in a bar.

"Listen, as much as I'd like to walk out of here right now with you, I need a minute." Artie glanced down at his jeans, and back up to Veronica's face. She realized he meant his body was having a *very* visible reaction to their kiss.

Veronica grinned, hoping to discourage any embarrassment he might have been feeling over something that felt like a bit of a compliment.

When they finally walked back to the hotel together, Artie reached over and held her hand in his.

In the hotel, they were about to part ways to their separate rooms, but before they did, Artie kept her hand in his, and pulled her toward him, "Come here."

She obeyed, and they kissed again, in the lonely and dimly lit hallway of a hotel.

Later that night, laying in her hotel room bed, all the fluffy, white bedding surrounding her, Veronica played back their kiss - scratch that, their kisses, over and over in her head. And the fact that he thought she was interested in William, her boss, her mentor. It occurred to her then, Artie had only made a move and kissed her *after* he confirmed that she was in fact not interested in her boss in that way.

Did that explain why he was reserved and stand-offish in the past? Is that why she was reading him as pretentious - because he suspected something, and kept to himself until he knew the truth?

What Veronica knew was that even though he considered for a moment that she might have been the type of person to entertain an inappropriate relationship with her own boss, she couldn't stop thinking about kissing him. About feeling his chest from the other side of his shirt. And yet she had to present to a conference audience the next day.

Veronica grabbed a pillow that was next to her and put it over her head, hoping to suffocate any lewd thoughts about Artie so that she could get some actual sleep.

Chapter 13

Veronica did not sleep well the night before. The nerves she felt leading up to her presentation only intensified as the night wore on and as it got closer to morning. She managed to finally fall asleep, but it was a restless sleep, not deep. As she slept, her mind feared she would sleep through her alarm, or that the alarm wouldn't go off at all, or that her phone battery would die even though it was plugged in. However, her phone battery did not die, her alarm went off as planned, and she did not sleep through it.

She rose out of the unfamiliar hotel bed to finally get ready, her eyes aching with lack of sleep, and dread in her stomach. It was one of the few times she styled her hair after washing it in the shower that morning. Veronica's usual modus operandi was letting it dry in waves by lunch time. She didn't have that luxury on a day she was set to speak in front of a live audience.

Fully dressed in the outfit she picked out, note cards in hand, Veronica sat on the hotel bed and flipped through her notes one last time. She didn't plan to use the note cards when on stage, but she wanted to be able to look through her presentation up until the last moment. She opted to wear a simple and comfortable black blouse, to keep her look simple and not distracting. But she paired it with a pair of copper pants, hoping to channel some of the bold energy they offered.

As the clock ticked, it was finally time for her to head to her session. She grabbed her bag, the hotel room key, and smoothed her hair with one last look in the large mirror by the hotel room door. And then she stepped out.

The walk from her hotel room to the conference room was a blur of faces and chatter that all meshed together. Veronica found a seat in the front row of the room among the rest of the presenters that were speaking in her session. She tried to steady her breathing, but all she could do was breathe just enough to keep the nerves in her stomach from turning into nausea.

She saw William slip into the room and take a towards the front. Their eyes locked and he gave her a silent thumbs up in assurance. She was glad to have him there, a friendly face in a sea of strangers. The room wasn't packed, and she was equally glad that it wasn't bare, either.

She scanned the people around William, recognizing a few faces from the museum, but there were two other people besides William that she had hoped to see. She didn't see Henry's infamous scowl, which would be surprisingly comforting in the many unfamiliar faces. Veronica had hoped that this would be an opportunity for her digitization work to shine, a way to convince him how valuable her process could be for the anthropology collection, like it had been for the botany collection.

Veronica took a big breath in and sighed. In addition to not seeing Henry, she didn't see Artie. She wasn't sure if seeing him would make her nerves skyrocket, or if having him there would be calming. She started counting her breaths: four counts in, four counts out, and told herself that she may never know.

The first presenter in the session took the stage and began their talk. Veronica was third on the list of presenters, out of ten. As the first presenter skipped to their next slide of data, Veronica could barely focus on the research. All she could think of was the process of breathing, and on her own presentation ahead of her.

Veronica's focus broke when she heard the door open, and she couldn't help but turn her attention to it. In walked Artie, who looked around the room for her face before he smiled and took a seat in the back. His chest was rising and deflating quickly, like he rushed to be there, and his hair was swept off his face.

She found out that the butterflies she felt when Artie was around didn't necessarily replace her nerves, but they sure did distract her from them.

Soon after, when it was Veronica's turn to take the stage, she tugged on her blouse mindlessly, finding comfort in feeling the soft fabric between her fingers. As she stood on stage, she looked at her slides, and then at the audience, the many pairs of eyes in her direction. And then she opened her mouth and spoke about her favorite place in the world: the botany collection at the museum.

The session was over, and Veronica felt an immediate release of tension leave her shoulders. She felt giddy and glad that it was done. Everyone stood to leave the room for the conference team to prepare the room for the next session and the presenters.

Veronica was making her way toward the exit doors with the crowd, when a young woman came up to her. Guessing her age, Veronica assumed she must be a graduate student.

"Hi, I'm Margot, I'm also a botanist, with a specific focus on neotropical taxonomy, like you," the girl introduced herself, sticking her hand out as a greeting.

"Hi Margot, I'm Veronica," she replied, accepting the handshake.

"Your presentation was so great. I'm taking classes at the university here in San Francisco. I wouldn't normally be able to attend this conference, but I was able to convince my advisor that it was valuable for me to come. I loved your presentation and how you're making specimens more accessible to scientists. I actually used one of your scans from your museum's collection in my research," Margot continued, her words dripping with enthusiasm.

Veronica felt so proud and flattered, thinking this must be what it felt like to work with the FBI to solve a murder with plants, like science royalty. "That's amazing, I'm so pleased to hear that. If you ever need to loan specimens for your research, or to visit the collections, please do reach out. I would love to show you the museum if you're ever in the Midwest."

Margot and Veronica spoke a little longer about neotropical biology, and when the room was nearly empty, Veronica wrapped up her convo with the young student and waved goodbye.

"You've inspired the next generation," William said, having waited for Veronica. "Congratulations, you did great."

"Thanks, William. She was so nice. I feel so accomplished, mostly because it's over, and because I got to speak to someone who has physically used our collections in their research because it's digitized."

"You were fantastic," Artie reassured her as he stood just behind her boss.

"I'm so relieved people showed up and actually listened," she replied.

"Of course they listened. I'm sorry I almost missed it. I came straight from the student competition session I judged this morning - I didn't realize it was on the other side of the conference center."

"I'm glad you made it," she shared honestly, a smile creeping on her lips that she couldn't resist.

"Don't forget, the museum staff dinner is tonight. See you later?" William asked them both.

Artie and Veronica nodded in unison, agreeing to be there. The group dispersed, but not before Artie gave Veronica a quick smile in return when William turned his back.

Chapter 14

They left the conference room, and their feet carried them to the registration area, unsure of where to go next. Veronica stared off into the distance, all the adrenaline from the day leaving her.

"Breathe, it's over," Artie commanded as he took her shoulders in his hands to bring her back to reality.

"Sorry, I'm still reeling from the presentation," Veronica said. "I'm going to need to change before I head out to dinner."

"Alright, meet you there?" he offered.

"I'll be quick, you can come with me," she said nonchalantly, her head still in the clouds.

All this tension had built up for the presentation, and now it was over. And while Veronica was feeling less anxious, there was still something brewing in her body that she couldn't put her finger on. The nerves in her stomach had settled now, but the butterflies hadn't left ever since the kiss they shared in the bar last night.

Artie followed Veronica to her hotel room for her to change before dinner. She let him in and motioned for him to take a seat while she rummaged through her suitcase looking for a change of clothes.

Veronica changed in the bathroom, slipping out of her business casual attire and into comfortable jeans and a capped sleeve t-shirt.

On the other side of the door, Artie glanced at the thin barrier of plywood that separated them. His thoughts turned dark, knowing what was happening on the other side, but imagining what else *could* be happening.

When Veronica came out, Artie wasn't looking at her, at least not right away. He was sitting on the edge of the bed, trying not to impede on her personal space, her sleeping space, and yet all he wanted to do was get closer to the sheets of her hotel bed.

He pulled his thoughts away from the image of Veronica changing her clothes, and his eyes left her bedsheets that he had been staring at. And he looked at her, the real her, right in front of him. And he wanted to touch her.

"This feels more comfortable. You ready?" she asked, still buzzing with adrenaline.

Artie said nothing, and while he didn't take a step forward, he did stand. And he stared. Her hair had fly-aways from a busy day, her white shirt was bright, reflecting the last of the day's light onto her face like a spotlight, and her jeans hugged her hips, tracing a line all the way down her legs in a way that made Artie jealous of how the fabric touched her.

"Veronica," he finally breathed.

"Yes, Artie?" She liked the sound of her name when he said it. She echoed his name with a grin. But he wasn't smiling.

"You are so beautiful," he replied, making her blush. "When I see you enter a room, I can't think of anything else. My name in your mouth is the best it's ever sounded; it makes me crazy. Your smile with your pointy canines stops me in my tracks. Your hair takes forever to dry after you wash it and I just want to be enveloped in it. Your passion for the work you do for science, your passion for anything, I could listen to you talk about that for hours. All I want is to know the curves of your body like braille. I want to be the fabric that flows in and around your thighs." After a beat, he ended with a pleading, "Can I kiss you again?"

"Don't make me wait any longer," Veronica stood where she was, and let him come to her.

He stepped closer to her immediately, eliminating the empty space between them. His hands started at her shoulders, holding her in place, taking her in. "I don't think I'll be able to stop once I start..." his pupils grew wider as he looked down at her chest, and then up at her lips.

She considered what she wanted, and touching him was certainly it. Her years of insecurities and her past relationships came flooding in. And yet, at the same time, she thought of all the pep talks Camilla had given her these past years. Of all the times Camilla has effortlessly just asked for what she wanted.

"Then don't stop," Veronica whispered, looking at his lips, wanting to claim them. He ran the back of his knuckles down the front of her shirt, where the fabric stretched and rippled in the middle of her chest.

A filthy smile stretched across his face, until it turned down, dark.

In unison, each of his hands made their way up her to neck, and she couldn't help but roll her head back at his touch. When his thumbs made it to her chin, the rest of his fingers pressed into the base of her neck and he swung her head back toward him, an inch away from his face. His hands stretched the length of her jaw, and then he zeroed in on his target.

They kissed slowly at first, as if asking permission to come out and play. And then in a guttural voice he simply said, "Veronica." When he opened his mouth to utter her name, her lips took the opportunity to open simultaneously. His tongue found hers and then she felt him kissing her like he was hungry.

All Veronica could think was, *aggressive.*

And then he gently sunk his teeth into her bottom lip, *aggressive.*

As much as she wanted it to begin already, she also never wanted it to end.

He must have felt it too because he groaned, "I don't have condoms on me." He closed his eyes, pausing, despondent.

"I'm on the pill," she replied, greedy for him to keep his promise, and not stop once he started.

In one slick movement, he untucked her shirt from her jeans, and slid her top up over her head. He moved her to the bed and once she was laying back, he kissed her mouth for a while before he slid her pants off. He planted kisses from her throat to where her panties touched her pelvis. His lips left wet marks, and the cool hotel air made his trail of kisses feel ten times more thrilling on her skin. Her skin prickled and she shivered.

"Are you cold?" Artie asked, pausing with his mouth near her panties. He instinctively ran one hand up and down her exposed thigh, generating warmth.

Hating that the kissing had stopped, and with it, the electric feeling, Veronica encouraged, "Don't stop."

He continued to make his way down and softly kissed the inside of her thigh. Veronica felt and heard the vibration of a grown in the back of his throat. She ached to feel him, his skin, closer. She reached down and gripped the edge of his shirt and tugged, freeing his torso from the fabric so that she could feel his skin against hers.

Breaking from kissing her thighs, Artie made his way back up to kiss her mouth. He slipped her bra off - gently, followed by licking and sucking her breasts - not so gently. His hands could barely handle touching his skin to a real, live wish.

"Fuck, Veronica," Artie managed to let out. As he paused from mouthing her nipples, he instead rested his cheek on the swell of her breast, gently brushing his lips back and forth across her sensitive skin.

"That's the idea," she mindlessly replied, earning a small laugh from him as he looked up at her from her chest.

She felt a heat deep in her pelvis, the need for his body to be closer than it already was, growing. He could sense her body ache toward him like a magnet, so he slipped his hand into the other side of her panties, and he touched her, feeling her body swell, soften, and give, little by little.

Veronica writhed below him, enjoying the moment, but in time, her need and heat rose. Needing and wanting him, she slipped her hands into his pants, reaching for him. Veronica stroked the length of him once, and then twice, her hand memorizing his shape and size. With his jaw dropped slightly, Artie pushed her hand away. He was already so far gone, and he didn't want to come undone yet.

With a soft, "Not yet," he continued to caress her with her panties on, and although he was taking his time, his own restraint was coming to an end. He was going to need to feel her, all of her.

Artie stood up and slipped her panties down her legs. She stayed in bed but propped herself up on her elbows. The sun was setting on the other side of the small hotel window, causing the light in the room to dim to a cozy evening glow, and simultaneously making her feel secure in her own naked skin.

"You, too," was all she said, pointing to the pants that he was still wearing, and the bulge that was very visible from her point of view.

Artie grinned, and he pulled both his pants and his boxers down in one, slow motion. When he was standing back up, his body showed his ache for hers.

Veronica got up from her position on the bed and stood right in front of him. He was taller than her, but she was tall enough. She barely touched him, except for putting her legs on either side of his dick, letting him rub right against her opening.

"Holy shit," he moaned and tilted his head back, barely able to look at her naked body while she stood like that in front of him, because he knew it would be over if he did.

Veronica put her hand through his hair, his waves long enough to slip between her fingers like silk. She kept his head back and planted kisses on his Adam's apple as it bobbed. She felt him twitch between her thighs. Like answering a prayer, she lifted one of her legs, sliding the inside of her thigh up along his hip.

Both of their heads faced down now, looking to bridge the gap, finally. A little clumsy, they found the way this puzzle fit together like every pair's first time. And when she went to guide him into her, this time, he didn't push her hand away.

They started slowly, a little at a time, and then he found himself entirely inside her, thrusting further and further.

"Holy shit," he stammered again. They were thrusting, but then Artie moved her body to the bed to get more comfortable and relaxed. He could tell he wouldn't be able to last much longer, but each position change made it last a little more.

"Holy shit," she panted right back to him.

"I don't want to leave. I don't want to go back to the city," Artie said into her throat, holding her hair and cheek in one of his hands.

"We can do this in the city, too." Veronica rocked her hips in time with his.

"But that means I'd have to stop doing this in order to get on a plane back there." Artie slipped his hand to polish her parts, while still thrusting into her.

Wrapped together like their bones belonged to each other's bodies, Veronica felt the moment when it was all too overwhelming and let herself come undone. He let himself follow her down into an abyss.

Attempting to steady her breathing, Veronica laid back on the bed. Artie laid next to her with his arm draped over her stomach.

The best part of her day was conquering speaking in front of a live audience at the conference. So far as she could tell, he was the best part of the night.

With the arm that was over her, Artie pulled her closer to him. And that's how they stayed, until the next morning.

Veronica's eyes slowly opened, her internal clock roused her, even in the different time zone. She registered that she was in her hotel room and the morning sun was coming in through the sheer curtains. Underneath the sheets she felt warm, and realized it was because Artie's sleeping body was right there next to her still.

She peered over at him, his body slowly rising and falling with the steady breath of deep sleep. A little bit of his bare chest peeked out from the covers, which reminded her of last night, and her pelvic ached for more at the thought of it.

Since he was still sleeping, Veronica slowly turned over to glance at the hotel room clock that sat on the bedside table. She must not have been slow enough, because as soon as she turned over, she felt an arm reach over her torso and pull her closer.

Artie enveloped his arm around her, nuzzling his nose in her hair as he brought her against his chest.

"Good morning," she said, smiling to herself. The only witness to her smile was the small reflection of the clock. It read 7:02 AM.

"Hi," he said softly inside her hair.

"It's seven," she reported, turning toward him a little.

"It's early," Artie kept his eyes closed, enjoying the ends of her hair falling across his face as she moved, tickling him.

"I'm an early bird, with a flight to catch."

With that, Artie reluctantly opened his eyes but wasn't disappointed when he saw her face. His eyes made their way down her torso, taking in her body in the morning light. His arms didn't release her.

Veronica leaned over and slowly planted a kiss on his lips before slipping out from his grasp. She dressed herself, brushed her teeth, and packed the last remaining items into her suitcase. Silently, Artie followed suit, dressing into his clothes that were strewn in various directions from the bed.

They both left the hotel room, and Veronica let the heavy door click loudly behind her. In the dim, quiet hallway, Artie faced her, and one more time, he placed each of his hands on her cheeks and brought her lips to his for a relaxed, morning-after kiss.

When the kiss broke, he brought his hands down, and took her suitcase from her hand. One of Artie's hands pulled her suitcase to the elevators, and his other hand casually grabbed hers to hold, the warmth of his fingers comforting in the cold, air-conditioned hallway.

At the elevators, Artie pressed the down button for Veronica, and the up button for himself.

"I'm going to head to my room," he explained. "My flight is later this evening."

Veronica nodded, unsure of what else to say.

"I'll see you back in the city," Artie said, just as one of the elevators chimed. The downward facing arrow next to one of the doorways illuminated, their faces turned toward it.

They shared one last kiss for that day, and Veronica silently hoped it wasn't the last kiss for good.

Chapter 15

Veronica turned her cell phone service back on once the plane touched down just outside of her city. She was returning home from the conference, and with the time difference, she had just a few hours before it was time to sleep and get up for work the next morning.

Her phone dinged with a handful of text messages coming through.

MOM: *Did you land yet???*

CAMILLA: *Text me when you're back in the city - let's get coffee! I want to hear how your presentation went.*

ARTIE: *Safe travels*

That last one gave her the warm fuzzies, and she stared at the screen at that message so long that her eyes went blurry.

Veronica texted her mom first, reassuring her that she was safely on her way to her apartment. Then, she scheduled coffee with Camilla before hopping on the train that arrived to take her back to the city.

Once she sat down on a seat, her suitcase taking up legroom next to her, she thought more critically about what to say to Artie. She wasn't sure what to reply, until she got home, and plopped her luggage down right in front of her apartment door.

She sunk into her couch, ready to take a shower, when she sent a reply to Artie.

VERONICA: *I just walked into my apartment. Ready to shower off the airplane germs.*

He texted back almost immediately.

ARTIE: *Are you doing that on purpose?*

She smiled at her phone coyly. Of course, she was, but she didn't want to give in too quickly.

VERONICA: *Doing what on purpose?*

ARTIE: *Making me think about you in the shower*

VERONICA: *Is it so bad?*

ARTIE: *When I'm thousands of miles away surrounded by strangers in an uncomfortable seat at the airport instead of being near a shower with you*

ARTIE: *Yeah, it's not great.*

Veronica tried to hold back her own smile, relishing in the feeling of being wanted, and wanting him back. Her stomach tumbled with butterflies, but the discomfort of nerves and flirting was a welcome feeling.

VERONICA: *Now I'm thinking about you being near a shower with me. So we're even.*

With that, she forced herself to drop her phone on the coffee table, and she made her way to a cold (or hot) shower.

The next morning, Veronica was heading back to work, but made plans to catch up with her best friend in the early morning over some coffee before heading to the museum.

They typically met at a coffee shop next to the train station that they both took to head downtown. But this time, Camilla suggested they meet at a new coffee shop in the downtown area. Camilla loved anything new and shiny.

Veronica arrived after Camilla was already there, waiting in line. Veronica loathed waiting in lines. She loved everything about city-living: how the city came alive with everyone heading outside during the first warm day after winter, how sharing public parks and public transportation with others made you patient, and all the free cultural community activities to be a part of throughout the year.

However, the one thing she hated about living in a city was the lines. The lines to get into the newest restaurants, the bars with covers, the pop-up events so popular that you had to wait before you could get in. Waiting in a line just because something was trendy was the one way that did not encourage Veronica to be patient.

Veronica joined Camilla in the queue of people, feeling bad for cutting the line that had formed behind her friend. Veronica gave Camilla a look to convey how displeased she was. But Camilla, the marketing maven that she was, only beamed at Veronica and said, "I hear there's a really delicious chocolate and peanut butter latte that they make."

Veronica rolled her eyes. After waiting close to twenty minutes in line for coffee, they received their drinks and headed to a small table in the corner that was also occupied by other patrons equally as excited as Camilla.

"Now tell me, how did the conference go?" Camilla said as Veronica plopped down into her chair, the only thing louder than her friend's voice was the scraping of Veronica's chair legs against the floor of the coffee shop.

Veronica did her best to not let her displeasure of having waited in a line first thing in the morning taint the rest of her day. She took a breath and gave her friend a synopsis of her few days at the conference, as well as her presentation itself, ending with, "I'm so glad it's over.

"I knew you'd be great! Do you think you'll do it again next year?"

"Honestly, I don't know if I'll submit a presentation. Maybe if they invite me back, but this whole choosing to be nervous thing may not be for me."

"Oh come on, I'm sure it will get easier and easier each time you do it. Don't be the one to hold yourself back," Camilla said.

"I can always count on you for a pep talk," Veronica replied. "In all honesty, I really was hoping that my presentation could influence the head of anthropology to accept volunteers to digitize their collection, but he didn't even show up to my talk."

"Have you talked to him about it?"

"Yes, of course, and he's insistent that the Anthropology Division can't have volunteers. Meanwhile every collection has had volunteers in one capacity or another through the years."

"Dang, I'm sorry he didn't show. How could he not come around to the digitization idea - you're the nicest person I know, you can convince anyone of *anything* with your kindness," Camilla said, nearly batting her eyes at her friend.

"Kindness doesn't get you far in the workplace. I wish I was more cutthroat." Veronica sighed.

"No you don't. Then you wouldn't be you."

"But I could be more like you. Confident and determined and strong."

"Well, I appreciate that you think of me that way. And I hate to be the one to break it to you, but you are all those things too. You just tie it all up in gift wrap and ribbons. My delivery is a little more,

'I just got this present from the store and I didn't even take the price tag off.'"

Veronica laughed, and then took the moment to warm her hands on her coffee mug, and let it sink in that maybe her friend was right. Maybe she was also confident and determined.

Camilla sipped her latte and closed her eyes in pleasure. After composing herself, she continued, "What about your boss? What did he think about your presentation? Maybe he could help convince the head of anthropology."

"He came to my talk, of course. But I didn't see him much after that, actually. We briefly talked, but my talk was on the last day, and I didn't make it to the last night's reception," Veronica added, bashfully.

"Were you too wiped after your talk to be social?" Camilla asked, sounding disappointed.

"Well, not exactly. There's been some... developments," Veronica smiled as she said it. The only thing to make her instantly forget about waiting in a line, was the mental image of Artie tilting his head back when her naked body touched his.

"Oh?" Camilla asked, her eyebrows coming closer together, "Also with work?"

"No, not really."

"What do you mean, not really?" Camilla was confused, and her frustration came out as an eager hand motion, as if to say, *hurry it up.*

"All that anticipation was built up and my presentation went well. And then Artie and I kind of celebrated, in a pretty intimate way, if you're picking up what I'm putting down?" Veronica stuttered. She looked around and felt bashful as she discussed her sex life with her closest friend at a coffee shop, surrounded by people taking photos of their fancy coffees.

Camilla's hands were clasped around her latte, and Veronica could tell at first that she wasn't following.

Until suddenly, Camilla's eyes widened and one of her hands that was wrapped around her mug came up to her mouth as her jaw dropped.

"Veronica Sterling is daring to entertain a workplace romance? I never thought I'd see the day," Camilla sounded equally surprised, excited, and downright scandalized. "Tell me everything, from the beginning."

"I don't think we have time for everything," Veronica said shyly.

"At least tell me who made the first move," her friend asked with puppy dog eyes, wanting all the details.

"Listen, I have to get to work soon. While this latte is absolutely delicious, it cut out twenty minutes of hot gossip. I promise I will spill all the details," Veronica tried to nip it in the bud, but Camilla's face fell, pleading for details. "But uh, he made the first move."

Camilla tilted her head back, enjoying a satisfying moment. "Yes!"

By stopping for coffee on the way to work, Veronica arrived a little later than expected, even having left early to accommodate the coffee date. She quickly said hello to some fellow staff on the way to her little office, popping her head into William's office to say a proper good morning.

"Have you recovered from the resounding success of your first presentation?" William asked as he pulled his glasses down from his nose.

"Yes, I have. But not recovered enough to agree to another one," Veronica joked.

"Not yet, at least," he replied with an understanding nod. "We missed you that last night, I was hoping to hear how it all went while it was fresh."

Veronica paused, unsure what to say. But then she found herself saying, without thinking, "I know, I stayed in. I felt drained."

She instantly felt bad for lying to her boss. Her mind raced with confusion, how did she get to the point of lying to her boss, the one person in the museum that she respected the most? She felt instant regret, and that if she needed to lie about what she was doing, then wasn't it wrong?

"Well, once you're settled back in, and recharged, let's discuss how it went for you," he said, interrupting her thoughts that spiraled.

Veronica nodded and quietly left his office.

Once she reached her office door, she saw that the mailbox was full. In it, among paperwork and mail, another flower. This time it was jasmine. *Cestrum nocturnum* was all that the label said. Night-blooming jasmine. The specimen was nearly dry, the tiny petals a little crisp at the edges, the strong, notorious scent mostly gone. It was at the bottom of the mail pile, perhaps sitting for a few days, she assumed.

Veronica wanted to get to the bottom of this, the third flower specimen. If William wasn't giving her unlabeled specimens, and the volunteers weren't placing them in her mailbox, she racked her brain on who else it could be.

She thought back to the missing loan request that was out of the collection for ten years. Could this be a loaned specimen?

Veronica checked the loan request tracking sheet on her computer, but there were no specimen loans that matched. She walked down the hall back to William's office and was surprised to find him still there, instead of in the botany collection.

Her knuckles tapped his door lightly, "Hey William, got a second for a question?"

He looked up from his computer at her, his blue eyes resting above the lenses of his glasses. "Sure thing."

"Do you still have that old loan request ledger?"

"I put it back in the botany closet on the lower level."

"Got it. I'm going to check it; I received another unlabeled specimen."

William was simply nodding as Veronica quickly left to take the staff elevator down a few floors to the old storage closets where archived binders and ledgers found their final resting place. The old loan request ledger was easy to find since William had just referenced it. Her eyes scanned through its pages, looking for any unaccounted-for jasmine, daisy, or violet specimens. She saw none, and even when she referenced the few remaining unaccounted specimens, none of them could have been mistaken for these species.

Disappointed it was not another mysterious loan request, and still confused as ever, Veronica left the closet full of ledgers and made her way back to the botany collection. She entered the staff elevator to ascend to the collections floor, swiping her badge before pressing the buttons absentmindedly. Before the doors closed, someone slid into the elevator with her.

It was Artie, already smiling as the doors closed behind him, leaving just the two of them on the elevator as it lurched into action.

"Good morning," she said, pleased to see him, snapping out of the daze of solving her mystery.

"Morning, Veronica," he replied, his voice low as he stepped closer to her, but not too close. He looked at the paper in her hands, and asked, "What do you have?"

"An unlabeled specimen," Veronica replied, holding the jasmine flower out for him to get a closer view. "Actually," she continued, "I'm not sure if it's a specimen from our collection at all."

Artie was close enough that all he had to do was reach just a few inches, and he could hook his finger into the belt loop on the hip of her jeans. And so he did, and he tugged her the slightest bit closer. Veronica wanted to resist, she didn't want to be intimate with someone at work, it felt innately wrong. And yet, there he was, tempting her. She felt herself stepping the slightest bit closer to him, leaning into his chest until her free hand touched the thin fabric that separated her fingertips from the skin of his torso.

She found herself quickly glancing up at the corners of the elevator and she confirmed that there were no cameras. Artie couldn't help but follow her eyes, and then he understood.

"We don't have to -" he started to speak and move slowly away from her, sensing her discomfort. But she slipped her hand under his shirt and up his back and pulled him closer to kiss him.

She initiated the kiss, and he leaned into her lips a little too eagerly. He felt her tense up only when he pushed against her and her back reached the elevator wall. As if his body knew it was only moments before the elevator doors were to open again, his hands went to make the most of it by reaching down to her thighs, spreading his fingers wide to grip as far as his thumbs would reach. He lifted her up, his hips pinned against hers, holding her higher and closer to him to savor each lick as their tongues met.

The kiss ended as quickly as it started. Their mouths were moving fast until their bodies felt the elevator start to slow. They pulled away from each other reluctantly. The collection sheet of the specimen was still in her hand, crumpled against his back as she held him to steady herself.

"Listen," was all he managed to say before the elevator stopped. He gripped her legs again and eased her back down to touch the floor.

They pulled away from each other like the same poles of two different magnets, repelling in unison with the elevator doors before them.

Rebecca, the library archivist, was on the other side of the doors, and then joined them on the elevator up to the collections.

Rebecca said hello to them quietly, looking at them from behind her glasses. After nodding his head politely to her, Artie turned back to Veronica, but kept his distance.

"Listen..." he tried again, with a long pause. Was he uncertain of *what* he wanted to say? Or trying to figure out *how* to say it all before the next elevator stop came? Figuring out what he *could* say, now that they had an audience?

The elevator slowed and was coming to Veronica's stop. Quickly, he went with, "Will I see you at happy hour?"

The floor stopped moving, the elevator chime sounded. Rebecca got off first but held her hand back over the sensor, holding the door for Veronica.

"Yes, I'll see you there," Veronica said to Artie as she walked past him. She felt the back of his hand graze hers as she moved toward the staff hallway. He felt warm, as always, and she already missed the feeling of his soft skin. She looked back to give him a smile, just to see his own close-mouthed smile already directed right back at her as he leaned against the far wall of the elevator. And then the doors closed.

Veronica had made it back to her office before she noticed the notification on her cell phone, a little red bubble telling her she had a text message.

ARTIE: *The elevator ride with Jane Goodall has been demoted to second best.*

Veronica smiled to herself. If he wanted to leave a lasting impression, he was succeeding. She could still feel the ache of his pelvis pressed against hers.

* Part Four *

Heather

Chapter 16

At the end of her workday, Veronica stayed late to prepare for the museum event where they bring members behind the scenes to see the collection items that are not on display, and to get a closer look at what each of the scientists were working on. It took place each year and it was her favorite event. She spent her evening mapping out where she wanted each of her volunteers, and what she wanted them highlighting to members about the collections, the department, and what they were actively researching.

Pilar was going to be in charge of the digitization room, with the DSLR camera setup and computers for uploading the high-resolution photos and entering label information into the database.

Veronica was planning to manage the larger display table that was going to be shared with the Division of Insects, to focus on the plant-insect relationship. She stayed late in the collections sorting through the drawers of botany specimens that relied heavily on insect pollinators, like crops.

After she sorted out the botany part of the Behind-the-Scenes event, she left the specimens out for the coming week and figured it was time to call it a night. She returned the specimens she would not be using to their cabinets, and then turned out the lights behind her.

Walking through the staff-only halls, she passed the other collections. The dim hallway lights barely illuminated the floor before her as she passed the wooden doors of the Division of Botany, Division of Insects, Division of Geology, and other names painted onto the glass embedded in the old wooden doors.

Each door was a thin barrier to a collection of natural history on the other side of it, rich with stories and meaning. Each record on the other side of the doors was an archive of the world that came before her, and each one felt more meaningful to her than she cared to admit. What was it about those specimens and objects, those one-of-a-kind artifacts that gripped her so desperately that she valued them so highly?

Veronica walked to the exit to take a ride-share home instead of the train this late at night. She was one of the few left in the building. Walking through the main hall to exit out a staff-only door, she saw someone from housekeeping riding the floor cleaner, back and forth, rhythmically through the space like a slow-motion pinball machine, polishing the limestone floor.

As she made her way through the halls, she immersed herself in the idea of the member experience. She thought of seeing the behind-the-scenes collection for the first time, knowing that only 1% of the museum's collection was on display in exhibition halls. And through the attendee journey, through the staff halls during the Behind-the-Scenes night, and through getting to know the staff parts of the museum that she took for granted, she felt an immense love she had for the museum and it's collection around her.

She was deep in thought while she walked to the exit, passing silent collection items, deep with years of history.

Chapter 17

When Veronica walked into Classroom B for that week's happy hour, her eyes went straight to Artie, picking him out from the small crowd due to his height. He stood with Frances, so Veronica walked right up to them, not even realizing that she hadn't grabbed a drink yet.

"Hey," she said to Artie and Frances with energy, "Happy Friday!"

"Happy Friday," Frances sang back.

"Let me get you a drink. Is beer okay?" Artie asked, while simultaneously walking toward the drinks area.

"Yeah," Veronica managed to say, appreciating that Artie noticed what she drank each week. She side-eyed Frances, worried that she might catch on to the familiar behavior.

"I heard the presentation went well! How do you feel?" Frances asked her as they waited for Artie to return.

"Glad to have it over with," Veronica sighed. "If there is a next time, I'm confident I'll feel even better about that one."

Frances and Veronica were talking about the rest of the visit to California, when Artie returned to cheers them both with their drinks. As expected with the nature of the work happy hour event, Frances was pulled away to another group that wanted her opinion on something.

With Frances leaving to talk to someone in the bird division, that left Veronica and Artie to themselves. Veronica looked around the room, gauging who was around them, and specifically, who was in ear shot. Classroom B was a small room, but thankfully the lively chatter bounced off the hard surfaces and was enough to drown out their conversation.

"Have you told anyone about us? Or this, whatever this is? Like, Henry?" she asked, hushed.

"No. Do you think it's something we need to disclose?" Artie said, unsure where she was going with this.

"No. I mean, I don't know. I really am not sure. William and I were discussing my presentation and he said he was disappointed that I didn't make it out that night to celebrate. And I lied to him. I didn't tell him I was with you, I said I stayed in because I was drained from speaking at the conference."

Artie nodded, soaking it in, the secret, what it meant. Then he shared, "That's not a huge lie. But I'm sure it didn't feel good to lie to your boss. Do you think he was suspicious?"

"I don't think so."

"I'm not purposefully hiding it from people, in general. But in all honesty, I have been hesitant to share our... developments... with Henry. I don't want to jeopardize my fellowship."

"I don't want to jeopardize your fellowship either, or my own reputation, or my position at the museum. And don't get me wrong, *I* was not disappointed that I didn't make it out of the hotel room that night," Veronica said. They shared a smile, each of them keeping their voices low and trying desperately to keep their hands to themselves.

"I don't want to hide it; I'd shout it if I could. More than anything, I want to show you off," Artie said, and then quieter, he added, "Can I take you out to dinner? A proper dinner?"

"Do you have time for that? With your postdoc?" Veronica asked, giddy at the idea of a proper date in their city, together.

"Yeah, I'll make time," was all Artie said, with a finality and certainty that put a little heat deep in her pelvis.

"Yeah," Veronica echoed, trying on the idea as it passed her lips. "Okay, I'd like that. Let's go out to dinner, together, in public. But maybe at the museum, we keep this between us?" she added, her voice dropping low, remembering their kiss in the elevator, and not loving the idea of potentially being caught together in an intimate moment where she worked.

"Whatever you think is best, this is your turf."

How does he do it? Veronica thought. *How does he say the right things?*

She stifled the urge to kiss him, knowing she wanted to keep it as professional as possible within the perimeter of her workplace.

She felt the impulse to touch him in whatever capacity she could, so she placed her fingers around his hand that held his beer. Her hand slowly caressed his as she steadily pried his can of beer from his soft grip. Keeping eye contact with him, which Artie was so good at, she took a sip of his beer, willing herself to focus on this six-degrees-of-separation kiss.

Artie's jaw dropped modestly, just enough for his tongue to subconsciously reach for his back molars. He ached to kiss her at this moment, too. And while she almost expected his eyes to fall to her lips, his eyes never fell from her gaze. He stared at her so intently, she began to wonder if he was aware that he was doing it at all. It very well may have been second nature for him.

She wanted to look away, but instead she handed his beer back to him after she took a sip. Then, she said, "You sure have some confidence being able to hold eye contact like that."

"I just really like looking at you."

The two chatted together, and with others. And soon, happy hour came to a close and many were saying their goodbyes for the weekend.

"Can I drive you to the train?" Artie asked Veronica, once they were alone.

They walked to the parking garage together, and as she took a seat in the passenger side of his car, she asked, "How far out of your way is the train station?"

"Not far," he replied, vaguely.

"Do you at least live in this general direction?"

"I assure you, I don't mind," and after a pause, Veronica still waiting for him to answer her question, he continued, "Yes, I live on the west side."

Veronica wondered where on the west side he lived, since she lived west too. But she kept her curiosity to herself.

While they drove, he held her hand, which felt somewhat surreal, but she relished in it all the same.

In typical Artie fashion, he parallel parked the car and got out to say goodbye to her.

This time, outside of his car as she stood from the passenger seat, Artie closed the gap between them, closed in on her, and gently pushed her up against the vehicle. He placed his thumb on her chin, with his pointer finger as support under it, and raised her lips up to his for a kiss.

"How about that date, tomorrow?" he asked when he pulled away.

Chapter 18

Veronica sat in the living room of her apartment, sipping on a hot cup of coffee that she had just made. The morning was cool and sunny, so she had her windows open, the city still quiet before the rest of the world was up and about. Her phone pinged in the kitchen, interrupting her woolgathering out the front window.

It was exactly who she thought it was, making plans for their first official date.

ARTIE: *Good morning. What do you think about Izakaya for dinner?*

VERONICA: *Morning. That sounds good. What time?*

ARTIE*: 7?*

VERONICA: *7 it is, see you then.*

ARTIE: *Do you want me to pick you up on my way?*

VERONICA: *No, it's not far from me. I can meet you there.*

She wondered if this is what it would be like if they were together. Making plans, seeing each other back-to-back.

Later that night, Veronica got ready and arrived for dinner. Artie was already there, waiting for her outside. As she walked up, they said hi to each other, and he leaned down to kiss her, while resting his warm hands on each of her arms. Even when they stopped kissing, they stood there for a moment, new to the rhythm of a date together.

"Ready to eat?" he asked, finally.

"Absolutely," she replied as he held the door open for her to walk in. She made a mental note of how chivalrous he was behaving, enjoying the attention.

As they waited for the hostess, he trailed his fingers down her neck. Since that night at the conference, Artie was touching her constantly. Now that he could touch her, it's all he wanted to do.

When the hostess came to the front and greeted them, Artie asked her for a table for two. But then, he paused, surveying the busy restaurant, and turned to Veronica. "Actually, do you want to sit at the counter instead?"

"Sure," she replied, open to watching the chefs make the sushi rolls in front of them and fire fried foods on the grill.

Artie turned back to the hostess and asked if that was possible, and the hostess motioned for them to follow her to the vacant sushi counter.

He took Veronica's hand and led her through the crowded restaurant, the cacophony of chatting around them. And while they weren't alone, the attention he gave her, his warm hand surrounding hers, made her feel like they were the only two people in the room.

Artie gently pulled out Veronica's stool for her, just a little, and he took a seat to her right.

They settled in with glasses of water and their napkins, until their elbows started bumping.

"Oh, we can't sit together, not this way at least," Veronica joked, eyeing him from the side.

"Too close for you?"

"You're left-handed! Our elbows will be black and blue by morning."

"Oh, I'm used to it. Unless you really want to switch?"

Veronica considered it, "No, it's alright."

"Good," was all he replied, as his left hand took her right one, and kissed it.

They ordered sake, various sashimi to start, and other small plates to share like takoyaki, kurage, and yakitori. Their food started coming in waves, and their conversation followed suit. As Artie started helping himself to various bites with his chopsticks, he gained the courage to ask what was on his mind.

"As a scientist, I'm sure you can relate, I like to have all of the data. So, tell me, how am I lucky enough to have met you while you are single?" Artie asked, trying to be coy and hide the small hint of insecurity that he felt surface at times.

"Oh, well, it's not so much luck. I've been single for some time now, so your timing had good odds," Veronica reassured him, fiddling with her chopsticks.

Artie saw her fidgeting, so he reached over and touched her wrist, swiping his thumb back and forth.

Veronica felt comforted and was curious herself. "And how am I lucky to have met you while you are single? You know, just to have all the scientific data."

He grinned. "I've dated. I've lived in this city since I was young." He took a breath before continuing, "The thing about living in the city you grew up in, the women I've been with, they move on, they move away. It's natural, many people seek to leave the place they've always known for a better opportunity. The grass being greener, and all that." His voice was quiet, but assertive. His shoulders shrugged, bouncing his own self-pity away as he removed his hand from her wrist.

"But not you? You didn't ever want to move away?" she asked.

"I'm still trying to figure out where I belong," he said plainly. "In any case, PhD candidates don't tend to have a lot of time for socializing or dating. It's the same now that I'm a postdoc. It would make sense that I would meet someone in the workplace."

They smiled at each other. Artie pressed on, "You can tell me about your past."

Veronica sighed. Her mind raced with her short dating history that close friends like Camilla knew all too well. And they knew the hurt that had come with that history, too. "There's honestly not much to tell. I had a boyfriend in college. But I moved to the city once I graduated." She paused to see if that stung, if it felt all too familiar for Artie, him being on the other side of that classic story. But he motioned for her to keep going.

"He didn't move to the city. Long distance didn't work. He met someone local. Tale as old as time," she continued, feeling the sting of being left. "Then I had a girlfriend for a short time, but we had different ideas for our futures, so that also didn't last."

Artie nodded, taking it in. "I'm glad to be sitting here now, with you," was all he said, and all he needed to say.

Veronica practically melted, then found herself shaking her head.

"What?" Artie asked, unsure of what she was thinking.

"I read you so wrong. I thought you were so conceited."

"Conceited? What on earth gave you that impression?"

"You seemed a bit standoffish, you avoided talking to me, refused to look me in the eyes. I thought you were going to be another Henry. Self-important. Elitist, maybe."

"Really? In the beginning?" Artie delved for more answers.

"I suppose so. Obviously, I came around," Veronica picked up her chopsticks, going in for another bite.

"Honestly, I was new. I'm slow to warm up to people. It goes back to that seeking a sense of belonging," he shared. "I wanted Henry to accept me, to think that I was like him, to feel that I belonged at the museum. And I absolutely was into you and was trying not to be."

Veronica smiled, trying not to let his silent pining get to her head. She playfully added, "Seems like your efforts failed. Couldn't quit me, huh?"

"No, I couldn't, could I?" His eyes looked up at her, a small smile on his lips.

"I'm sorry I judged you." Veronica looked at him plainly, truly feeling remorseful for making assumptions about him.

Artie shrugged his shoulders, "My mentor was a bit like Henry. Could be elitist in the scientific community. I judged him too, until I understood him."

"That doesn't make it right," was all Veronica replied.

Artie nodded his head, knowingly. After some time, he asked, "Girlfriend, huh?"

"Does that bother you?" Stunned, Veronica sat a little farther back in her seat.

"Of course not," he reassured her. "Surprised, that's all."

Veronica took it in for a minute, feeling how vulnerable he had just been while sharing, so she shared some of her own past, "She adored my body when I loathed it the most. When your boyfriend meets someone else, insecurities pop up, even if I knew I wouldn't have changed a thing about the choices I made."

Artie reached over, seeking her hand. Once he had it, he said, "Your body is extraordinary. Remarkable. Stunning. Marvelous."

He took her hand and raised it to his mouth, kissing it, and holding it. When she moved her hand from his mouth to hold his cheek, he leaned into it, seeking the closeness.

Veronica enjoyed the moment, feeling warm and fuzzy with the sweetness of his intimacy. And yet, there was something still bothering her about the question he had asked her when they were at the conference. As sweet as he was toward her, he only started showing physical intimacy when he confirmed that she wasn't romantically involved with William. What troubled her the most about this was that he thought she might be the type of person.

"Can I ask you something?" she prodded, drawing her hand away from his face.

"Of course," he said with barely any breath.

"Your accusation - the one where you thought I would ever consider an inappropriate relationship with my boss - how could you think I could be that kind of person?" she asked, earnestly.

Artie sighed, unsure where to begin. "You have to understand, I'm a postdoc. I come from academia. Academia attracts the worst sort of smug, superior elitists in existence."

"And?"

"The number of inappropriate relationships would astound you. Students would babysit for their advisors. And yes, they would absolutely sleep with their advisors, their professors. And trust me, it isn't always about advancing their own careers."

Veronica considered it. After some silence, she said, "I would never have babysat for any professor I had."

"Because you have boundaries. But the power dynamic at play, the coercion that happens inadvertently. After a while, it was no longer surprising when I heard about it. As you can see, I became hardened to it. I'm sorry I ever thought you would consider something like that with William. I know you better now. I know that you would never. I see now how much respect you have for him, and even how much respect he has for you."

"And you?"

"Me?"

"Would you ever?"

"Absolutely not. I would never engage intimately with a professor or an advisor of mine." After a moment he considered that many of his professors and his own advisor were men, and he added, "Regardless of their gender."

Artie was hoping it would lighten the heavy topic between them. But Veronica's expression didn't change.

"And if you were the professor?" she asked plainly, looking directly at him.

"Never," he said, succinctly as he held her eye contact.

At that moment, the chefs on the other side of the counter finished making the last of their food and placed a platter of yakitori in front of them.

Veronica sighed, ready to change the subject. "Well thank you for explaining that to me. It was bothering me, so I felt like I needed to bring it up."

"I'm glad you shared. I'm here to listen to anything you have to say."

Veronica served herself some skewers of meat from the platter in front of them.

"This might be a good time to tell you…" Artie started to say. Veronica's eyes widened and she stopped what she was doing. "My parents invited you over for dinner next weekend. If you can make it."

"Oh," she let out the air she was holding in. "They know about me?"

"Yes," he replied, taking a bite of a skewer to keep his mouth busy, almost like he wouldn't have to answer if his mouth was full. "Last time I saw them was before the conference. I might have mentioned you." Artie looked at her, catching her eyes to gauge her reaction. When she blushed and smiled, he smiled too. She liked that he talked about her; she liked it a lot.

"Okay," she said. "Next weekend? I can make it."

"Okay," Artie mirrored. "I'll pick you up."

At the end of the meal, they stepped outside and started to say their goodbyes.

"Thank you for dinner," she said, standing close to him.

"Of course." He held her hands with his, and he leaned down to kiss her.

"As much as I don't want to say goodbye, I should get home."

"I can drive you, unless you're taking the train?" he offered.

"The train station is only a block away," Veronica insisted, pausing with the lingering question of 'what's next?' in the air. "I'd invite you over, but Camilla is moving tomorrow, and in the morning, I'm helping her pack and bring over some of her valuables to her new place."

"I get it, you don't have to explain the reason. I'll see you at the museum this week."

Veronica warmed knowing he didn't press the matter. And she felt warm the entire walk to the train, knowing that Artie watched her the entire way until she disappeared from view.

Chapter 19

Veronica woke up the next morning with warm and fuzzy feelings of a date gone well. And at the same time, she couldn't help but want to spend more time with Artie already.

She told herself she had some work to do, which included helping her friend move, like she committed to.

When Veronica arrived at Camilla's former apartment to help, Camilla was holding two to-go cups of coffee and already buzzing with excitement.

"I've been up since six this morning, packing, and this is my third cup of coffee," Camilla said as she smiled wide.

"You were still packing as of this morning?" Veronica replied, incredulously.

"Everyone always has more stuff than they realize!" Camilla defended, before showing her friend the last bit she needed help with.

Veronica helped her pack the last few necessities that didn't end up in boxes for the movers, and they made their way to Camilla's front porch to call a ride-share.

"I wish we knew someone with a car," Camilla complained as she carried the last of her valuables, suitcase, and other immediate need items out to the curb before she opened her ride-share app. The "last few items" that Camilla had promised Veronica would only be a handful, turned out to be a few more things than expected.

Veronica plopped Camilla's box of skincare onto the sidewalk in front of her when it clicked. "Uh, I actually do know someone with a car."

Camilla eyed her, incredulous. "And you're only *now* saying something?"

"It didn't occur to me before this moment! I haven't known him that long," Veronica contemplated if she could even ask Artie for a favor for a friend of hers that he had never met.

"Ohhh," Camilla smiled, catching on that Veronica was talking about Artie. "Well, are you going to call him? Or do I need to call a ride?"

"Ride-share. This is so last minute," Veronica protested. She wanted an excuse to see him, but at the same time, she wondered if it was too early to ask for these kinds of favors. The helping-your-friend-move kind of favors. "I mentioned to him yesterday that I was helping you move today, and he didn't offer to help."

"You saw him yesterday?"

"Yes, we got dinner."

"Come on, you're going out on dates, you can totally cash in on a favor like this."

"Things are progressing, but I don't really know the status of it. I'm supposed to keep it under wraps at work but at the same time, I'm supposed to meet his parents next week," Veronica said, confused.

"You're going to meet his parents?" Camilla asked in disbelief, furious at her friend for withholding new details. "If you don't call him, I will."

That's what Veronica loved about Camilla, she was stubborn and headstrong and believed fiercely in working toward getting what she wanted.

"Fine. It doesn't hurt to ask," Veronica said, mostly to herself. In an effort to avoid Camilla being the one to ask Artie for a favor, Veronica dialed his number and walked a few feet away from her friend.

Artie picked up on the second ring and sounded a little out of breath when he said, "Hey, you."

"Hey Artie, are you busy?"

"Right now?"

"Yeah, I know it's last minute -"

"I'm not busy, what do you need?"

"Well, you know how I'm helping Camilla with her move?" Veronica squinted one eye, bracing to humble herself to ask.

"Do you need some muscles?" Artie teased.

"No, actually," she laughed. "It's not your body that I am asking for. It's actually - your car?" Veronica's voice went up an octave at the end, hoping to soften the request in the event he said no.

Artie hummed before he said, "I see. Well, it's a package deal. I can bring my car, but I'll be there to help the two of you carry whatever you need to transport."

"We'll take it." Veronica looked back toward Camilla, who was scanning her face to read what the verdict was. Veronica gave an affirmative thumbs up, and Camilla nearly did a jump kick in the air.

"Text me the address, I'll see you soon," Artie said before he hung up.

A short time later, Artie pulled up and parked his car as close as he could to Camilla's apartment, the moving truck blocking most of the street. When he got out of his car, Veronica spotted him from Camilla's porch, and waved him over. He was wearing a university t-shirt, and soccer shorts that showed more of his tan thighs than she expected to see. His hair was a little damp, his waves clumping together more than usual, heavy with moisture.

"Were you working out?" Veronica asked, somewhat surprised as he got closer.

"I was playing soccer, actually," he replied, climbing the porch steps to meet them, confidently taking them two at a time, eager as if he was impatient, yet confident at the same time.

"You said you weren't busy," she tsked.

"Practice was nearly over," he said with a hint of a shrug.

Veronica wasn't sure of the protocol. Should she kiss him hello, hug him? Do nothing?

Before Veronica could make a decision on how to greet him, Camilla inserted herself, and reached out her hand. "Hi, I'm Camilla, thanks for coming to the rescue."

Artie shook her hand, and said, "I'm Artie, happy to help." Then quickly, without fanfare, Artie leaned his face down to be closer to Veronica's as he claimed her lips with his in a soft kiss, "Hello."

"We'll be back!" Camilla interrupted as she shouted to the movers that were in and out of her apartment handling the larger items like her bedroom set and couch.

Camilla took charge, and immediately became familiar with Artie, she pointed to her boxes and bags of valuables that she and Veronica planned to move themselves. "There are more boxes than I thought, but if you could help us load these into your car and drive us to my new place, we'd be super grateful."

"You got it," was all he said, grabbing a box and multiple bags in one go.

Veronica grabbed a smaller box and was about to follow Artie to his car, when Camilla stopped her friend.

"What?" Veronica asked, trying to read her friend's facial expressions.

"Have you been downplaying the developments of this relationship?" Camilla asked, a broad smile on her face.

Veronica rolled her eyes and shifted the box in her hands, "No, I've told you everything."

"Going on dates, kissing hello, traveling together -"

"Both of us attending that conference hardly qualifies as traveling together," Veronica interrupted.

"Meeting the parents?" Camilla said seriously as she searched her friend's face. Veronica suddenly felt like Camilla could see everything, every feeling, and every thought.

Veronica's eyes quickly darted to Artie in the distance, as he started arranging the boxes and bags in the trunk of his car. She looked back to her friend, and said, "I haven't liked anyone this much in a long time."

"I know," Camilla said as she nodded sympathetically.

"Is it just because it's kind of forbidden? A workplace romance? He works in the Anthropology division, for heaven's sake," Veronica said, almost in disbelief at herself.

"Can you get any more self-aware?" Camilla laughed. The sound caused Artie to look over from the distance. But Veronica only stared at the cardboard box in her hands.

"Let yourself enjoy something good. You deserve it," Camilla said, rushed and hushed.

They both sensed Artie approaching the front porch for more boxes to bring to his car. Between the three of them, they were all able to carry the rest of the boxes to his car in a few more trips. And Camilla couldn't help but notice that Artie left one of his hands free to gently rest on Veronica's lower back as they walked down the porch stairs.

Chapter 20

The DEI committee had their next monthly meeting on the ground floor of the museum. Spring was coming to an end, and the summer internships were about to begin.

"One of the interns that applied has an interest in repatriation, and this could be a great opportunity for them to learn how our museum consults with indigenous communities and returns necessary items. I know that wasn't one of the original intern positions proposed by the various divisions, but I think it could be a great opportunity for both the intern and the museum," the head of the committee said.

"Should we connect with Henry about what capacity he could use an intern for the museum's repatriation efforts?" Frances asked.

"He really is so busy, he could definitely use some help managing all aspects of the division," another committee member chimed in.

Veronica looked around to gauge the faces around the table, and then she said, "What if we worked with the new fellow that is in the department, Artie? He might have more time to manage an outline of duties for an intern. And he might even be able to convince Henry about this opportunity better than we can."

The head of the committee nodded and said, "That's a start. Veronica, why don't you connect with the new fellow and see if you can get some buy-in. If we do some upfront work with Artie, it might alleviate any additional workload that Henry is hesitant to take on. Can you schedule a meeting with Artie?"

Veronica's stomach flipped with the idea that they could work together on something meaningful. It was an excuse to spend more time together. But then, Veronica questioned how she got herself involved in this. It occurred to her, now that they were to be working together on a project, technically, that perhaps it would be a conflict of interest after all.

The meeting ended, and Veronica moved slowly to gather her things. She saw Frances heading out the door, saying goodbye to some others, and Veronica decided to catch up.

"Hey, Frances," Veronica called after her. They walked together back toward the staff elevator and found themselves passing the anthropology lab. A large viewing window was cut-out in the exhibitions area, so that any museum attendee walking through the hall could view the artifacts that the team were actively working on. Instead, Artie and Henry sat at their individual workstations, a placard on display of the object currently in their care.

Artie and Veronica caught each other's eyes through the glass as she walked past, and the thrill of new romance swirled in Veronica's stomach. As she looked away, a smile formed on her lips, and out of the corner of her eyes, she saw one mirrored on his.

Once they were in the elevator, Veronica asked, "Can I ask you something a bit personal?"

Frances' eyes narrowed a little and she said, "Yeah, of course."

"Can I ask you your opinion on office romances?" Veronica nearly whispered, even though they were alone in the elevator together.

"Oh, wow," Frances stuttered. She paused before continuing, "Is this for a friend? Or for a *friend*?"

Frances ended her question with a wink, and Veronica could barely hold it together. She let out a laugh that quickly turned into a blush.

"Point taken," Frances said. The doors of the elevator opened, and they walked together to the PR office. "Listen, who am I to judge? If you're looking for my advice, just don't let it get messy."

Veronica nodded slowly, flipping the definition of "messy" over and over in her head, dissecting it like a specimen study skin in the Bird Division. "In that case, I might need a favor."

Frances stopped walking, and not because they had made it to her office. Veronica watched her colleague's face change as she slowly put it together. "I think I need you to spell this out for me, before I make any incorrect assumptions."

She went to open her mouth to explain but was stopped by Frances pulling her into the PR office and shutting out the hallway and beyond.

Veronica steadied herself, and quietly said, "I don't think I should approach Artie on the DEI Committee internship. It may be a conflict of interest to work that closely with him on one of the committee's initiatives. And I don't want to risk it getting *messy*, like you said."

Frances nodded as she put the pieces together, "I'm glad you told me. Does anyone else know?"

Veronica shook her head.

"No problem, I'll move the discussion forward with Artie. I've got this. I've got you," Frances reassured her colleague, her friend.

"What about the committee?" Veronica worried.

"What about them?"

"I don't want it to look like I dropped the ball on something I was tasked with."

"Leave it to me. I'm sure I can come up with something. I'll schedule the meeting with Artie, and if anyone asks, I'll say that you couldn't make it to the meeting last minute and asked if I could fill in. Or you're tied up with other department tasks that are priority right now and can't take on one more thing. Or that your cat died -"

"I don't have a cat," Veronica solemnly interrupted.

"Perfect! Then it won't be suspicious!" Frances joked, finally turning Veronica's upset stomach into a fit of laughter.

This time it was heather. It was at the top of the mail pile, and whoever placed it there must have just come by. The specimen, *Calluna vulgaris*, was pink and long. It was a heather flower, a common enough sight, which prompted her to consider why in its scientific name, the species was *vulgaris*.

Veronica was getting ready for the upcoming Behind-the-Scenes event for members of the museum, and did not have time to seek out the source of the mystery specimens. She barely looked at the rest of the label before putting it off to the side with the other specimens that had found their way to her mailbox. She mentally told herself that she would come back to them when things calmed down in her department.

"Future Veronica's problem," she muttered to herself, taking the pile of specimens, and putting them in a drawer of her desk, protecting them from the little bit of light that made its way through her small office window.

❀ Part Five ❀

Marigold

Chapter 21

It was the night of the Behind-the-Scenes event at the museum, and Veronica was equally excited for her favorite event of the year, as well as nervous for it to begin and go off without any issues.

In the Division of Botany, Veronica setup various displays for members to see, touch, and talk to the various staff and volunteers. As the members walked by the various collection cabinets full of specimens ranging from economic botany to plants and fungi, they would end in the hallway that would lead them to the Division of Insects. A natural segue from botany to entomology, Veronica planned to be stationed there with the Division of Insects Collections Manager, Maude, who hadn't arrived yet, to host an entire display on the plant-insect ecosystem.

Veronica was set up, and ready to go with about a half hour to spare before members were let in for the event. With all the planning that went into the displays, the staffing, and the creation of the member experience, Veronica was eager to get the night started - and over with.

As Veronica waited, Frances came by with the museum photographer to capture photos for press releases and media posts about the event.

"This looks great!" Frances boasted to Veronica as she looked over the display of plant specimens that relied on insects for pollination. The photographer clicked away, snapping shots of the table, the specimens, and even the staff interacting. "I'm making my rounds to each division before the attendees enter to get close-up photos of each display. Want to join me?"

"Sure - I have a little time before we get started," Veronica replied, excited to see what the other departments had worked on.

"I've already walked through the collections on this floor, we're headed to check out Anthropology next," Frances said.

Veronica tried not to react, but she couldn't help but falter at the mention of Artie's department. It was a beat before she replied quietly, "In that case, maybe it's best you head on without me."

Frances guessed what Veronica was alluding to. She angled herself to face Veronica, blocking the photographer from their conversation as he continued to snap photos of the specimens on display. "Are you avoiding him? Is this crossing into messy territory?"

"No, I'm not avoiding him. No one else at the museum knows except you, so I'm just trying to keep professional boundaries while also respecting that looping you into a secret that you didn't ask for could make things weird for you," Veronica explained through nearly a whisper.

"I hear you, but you should be able to just be yourself, at work *and* in your personal life. It seems like you've gone through great lengths to ensure there are no conflicts of interest. And yet, why do you look so stressed?" Frances pushed, reading the pained look on Veronica's face.

The botanist took a breath to calm her nerves, which she obviously wasn't doing a great job of, "He is very concerned with his fellowship, and rightfully so. And I don't want this to be a conflict of interest for the work I do at the museum, as well as within the committee."

Frances' eyes glazed over. Her eyes focused on the distance, on nothing at all as she processed the information Veronica was sharing. "How long has this been going on?" she finally asked her colleague, her voice even quieter than before.

"I suppose about a month."

"A MONTH?" Frances nearly shouted, and Veronica's spine straightened as she looked around to confirm that they definitely had the attention of the photographer now.

He took a hint, "I'm going to head to the restroom. Frances - meet you in the Anthropology collections area?"

Frances nodded with a polite smile, and as soon as he was out of sight, she pressed Veronica, "You've been dating him an entire month and are only sharing this with me now?"

"We haven't been *dating* for a month, more like just talking and seeing each other kind of a situation."

"This situationship has been going on for an entire month and you're only telling me now," Frances tsked, "I thought we were closer than that."

Veronica could hear the hurt in her colleague's voice. She had a point; they were closer than just coworkers. They were hired around the same time at the museum and had worked together for a number of years now. Veronica had been so caught up in her own world that she didn't stop to think of her other relationships in the museum, and how those themselves had crossed from working relationships to personal relationships without fanfare, without causing Veronica this much stress.

Veronica opened her mouth to apologize for the oversight when they were joined by Artie. Always knowing when to make an entrance.

"I forgive you," Frances said softly with a smile, and then she walked away to where Artie entered. "Hey Artie, I was just heading down to Anthropology to take some photos with our photographer. See you there?"

"Sure. Henry is there now, I'll head back soon," Artie replied.

Frances left them with a knowing smile on her face, and Veronica made a mental note to educate her on her poker face later.

That left just Artie and Veronica at the display. Artie started with a half-smile, "Hi."

"Hi," Veronica replied. "What brings you here?"

"Just thought I'd come see you and see what the Division of Botany has for the event tonight."

Veronica looked around her, "Well, the botany volunteers are stationed throughout the collections area -"

"I saw," he interrupted. "I was looking for you."

"I'm partnering with Maude, in the Division of Insects. So I'm here," she explained. "We have some crossover of specimens for the event: an entire plant-insect ecosystem display."

"Mind if I stick around a little while?"

"Won't Henry mind managing the Anthropology collection all on his own?"

"He hasn't minded before, has he?"

Veronica gave a quick laugh, noting how Artie teased the fact that Henry refused the help of volunteers or support staff in his division.

"Members will be arriving any minute now," she offered as an escape.

"I'll only hang around a little while, then I'll head back," he replied. "Besides, I want to see what you've been working on."

Maude from the insect division joined Veronica, and she introduced the two new faces to each other. Families started pouring into the collection areas, free to roam as they pleased, different staff and volunteers stationed throughout the staff-only floor to help them find their way from display to display, division to division, and even to the restrooms.

A family stopped by in front of the display of plants and insects on the tables in front of them. The small children's eyes were wide as they began to look at the colorful butterfly pollinators that were perfectly pinned in their unit trays within the glass-top collection drawers.

"Are those real?" a boy, about five years old, asked while pointing to the various blue morpho butterflies that were pinned to show off their metallic blue wings, as well as some displayed upside down, showing their wings that could camouflage them against a brown branch when closed.

"Yes, they are real. We call them specimens when they are displayed like this, so that we can study them, and learn from them," Maude, the insect collections manager explained effortlessly, switching into age-appropriate language.

"What are they doing in there?" The little boy asked another question but was interrupted by his older sister before he could get his answer.

"Are they dead?" She looked to be a year or two older, her eyes not as wide with wonder like her brothers.

"Well, yes," I could hear Maude's mind calculating how to best describe dead specimens to elementary aged kids with their parents nearby. "Butterflies like these blue morpho ones can live for about three or four months. However, many butterfly species only live two to four weeks. With their short life span, they spend their time catching many winds to enjoy as many flowers as they can. In turn, they help pollinate plants, which means they help carry seeds from plant to plant."

Maude was perfect in her description, Veronica could see it both in the children's faces, and the parents.

Veronica took the opportunity to chime in, "These plants here depend on pollinators like butterflies to grow. They depend on each other, really. Butterflies need the plants for nectar, and plants need the butterflies to spread the seeds."

The curious children continued to ask questions about the insects, as well as the plants, and Veronica chimed in here and there with facts about flowers she thought the littles would find interesting.

Off to the side, Artie mindlessly helped people find their way to the display as they milled about the floor. And yet, he tuned in to hear the conversations the two women were having with the museum members.

As the family walked away, leaving their display area empty for a moment, Maude said, "Makes you really appreciate living your life to the fullest, right? Knowing some creatures as beautiful as butterflies have such a short time on earth."

Her eyes drifted beyond the display in front of them, focusing mid-range, deep in thought.

"You give them a second life, by having them here for the public to learn about the world around them," Veronica offered kindly.

"I don't know, I think it's more special that these butterflies lived such a short time. And yet think about all that they accomplished, all the plants they must have pollinated, all of the winds they caught - like Maude said," Artie said, smiling. He added, finally, "I think it makes them more beautiful that they came, they existed, and the next generation will simply go on to do the same thing."

Veronica digested his point of view. But in her head, it sounded more melancholy than she thought he meant. She didn't have to linger on the thought long before another group of members came through to look at their display.

Having spent enough time avoiding his own division, Artie quietly said goodbye to both Maude and Veronica. He slipped down the hallway past Veronica to make his way back to the Anthropology collections, but not without softly running his hand across her waist as a goodbye.

The next morning, Veronica made her way back to the museum. However, being that she was just there the night before for the event, she took her time getting up, taking the morning slow, and rolled into her office closer to lunch time.

The museum strategically avoided morning meetings the day after the Behind-the-Scenes event, giving everyone that worked a chance to spend more than just a few sleeping hours at home in between the back-to-back days.

Veronica spent her first hour at the museum cleaning up the herbarium after the event, bringing specimens back to their appropriate storage cabinets. She organized the research stations to no longer be public displays, but instead back to how they usually look: a little cluttered, a little lived in, and a lot more bureaucratic and less welcoming.

In the midst of her morning of tidying up, Veronica's phone pinged.

ARTIE: *Need fresh air. I'm going for a walk along the lakefront path. Join me?*

Veronica smiled to herself and immediately checked her calendar to ensure she had time before her afternoon meeting.

VERONICA: *I've been in the Division of Insects today and I can still smell the naphthalene in my nostrils. Fresh air sounds perfect.*

ARTIE: *Hope it smells better than the flesh-eating beetle colony. Meet me at the hot dog stand near the north entrance.*

Veronica made her way to the hot dog stand, and could easily pick out Artie, leaning against the stone railing, tall among the crowd of tourists taking photos and eating hot dogs.

"What were you doing in the Division of Insects today?" Artie asked as they walked north along the path, the lake to their right, and the city skyline to their left.

"I was taking back some botany specimens they had from the member's Behind-the-Scenes event. But we started chatting and our discussion turned into how we could build upon it for next year. There was a lot of interest in it from our members," Veronica replied, keeping pace with Artie, his long legs taking him faster along the path.

"That's great. It's nice to see different divisions working together."

"It is, isn't it," Veronica smirked, silently teasing about his boss' ability (or lack thereof) to work with other departments.

"What if anthropology and botany work together next year?" Artie offered, looking sideways at her to gauge her reaction.

Veronica considered it thoughtfully and replied, "What do you have in mind?"

"Well, what about a display on ethnobotany, how people use plants? I'm sure there's a ton of specimens in the botany collection that have been used by Indigenous people. And having artifacts from the anthropology collection to compliment them, that could tie the narrative together, giving attendees a visual depiction of the people that used them, and how."

"I think we could do something with that. I like that idea, Mr. Ribeiro," Veronica replied, looking over to him. She smiled, but it faded quickly as she continued, "You'll probably need to put the idea in Henry's head now, before your fellowship is over. I don't see him being as agreeable to the collaboration next year without you."

Artie nodded and gave a playful sigh, but eager to change the subject, he said, "Camilla seems nice."

"Nice? Or authoritative?" Veronica wondered what he really thought of her, considering it was the first time he met her closest friend.

"She commands attention. Like I said, it's nice. Refreshing to meet more strong-willed women."

"Thank you again for helping with her move. We had planned to call a ride-share, but Camilla insisted I ask. As if that's what friends with cars are for."

"Friends?" he questioned. His step faltered for a moment, but he continued walking without a glance over to Veronica.

"Or?" she stuttered, wishing she had something confident and witty to say to him.

"Veronica," his voice was low, "I don't invite *friends* to dinner at my parents' house."

"Well, then we're dating? Going on dates?"

"Whatever you're willing to do with me, I'll take it."

Veronica laughed.

"Did that sound too desperate?" he asked, one corner of his mouth ticked up.

"No, no. I was just picturing the things I want to do with you," she offered instead, an image of them together on her hotel room bed flashed in her mind.

"A laugh is not a good sign," he offered.

Veronica's cheeks went pink, and it could have been because of the cool wind off the lake, or it could have been because she knew she was about to say, "Some people laugh at uncomfortable moments. And having a lewd thought would be an uncomfortable moment."

Artie looked over to her and just smiled at her honesty. Meanwhile, Veronica was feeling hot in her attempt to be bold, and she picked up her hair from the back of her neck to cool down. She wondered if Camilla always felt this way when she said whatever was on her mind.

His eyes gazed over to the lake, focusing on the horizon as they walked. Veronica's eyes mindlessly followed his.

"Did you ever do any field work?" Artie asked her, his mind traveling across the lake to a memory of his own. She was glad to have him change the subject before her cheeks turned any pinker.

"Yes, in Costa Rica. But I would love to go to Brazil one day."

"Is that so?" he replied, coyly.

"Thirty percent of the world's remaining rainforests are in Brazil alone. Tropical forests hold about fifty percent of the world's biodiversity," Veronica replied, and he stared at her blankly.

"Neotropical taxonomy is my specialty, remember?"

"I remember," he said solemnly. "Then you should go. To Brazil, that is."

"It was a little easier to get around Costa Rica with my high school level of the Spanish language."

"Portuguese is very similar to Spanish, I'm sure you could pick up some key phrases to get around."

"Like what?"

"Practical phrases like... my grandmother is always asking me if I am hungry, 'Está com fome?'"

"Ah yes, good phrase to know, in the event that I meet your grandmother," Veronica joked with a smile.

But Artie didn't smile. He softly said, "We'll get there."

His quiet confidence had a warmth spread throughout Veronica's body. She didn't want to focus on what that feeling was, so instead she got practical, "You're going to have to translate my field work packing list for me. What phrases should a botanist know?"

"Let's see... Plant is easy, plantar. Tree is árvore, leaf is folha. And flower - flower is flor. Though my favorite phrases to teach people are the curse words."

"When would I ever need to use curse words?" Veronica exclaimed, her voice increasing an octave.

"You never know," he smirked, before adding, "Although, you know what one of my favorite Portuguese words is?"

"Tell me," she insisted, taking the bait.

"Saudades. It loosely can be interpreted as 'I miss you,' somewhat of a sign off or statement to someone. But it means so much more," he paused, sitting in his feelings. Then, he continued, "More accurately, it would translate better to 'You are missing from me,' which I find more poetic."

Veronica swooned. She felt pale in comparison. Not only was he a postdoc scientist who was awarded a fellowship, he also spoke another language, he wrote poetry, and he made an effort to see her. And yet, she couldn't find herself just letting go.

"I like that one too," she said, staring at the horizon of the lake, in order to not be staring at him.

Chapter 22

They had said goodbye on the lakefront, and Artie discreetly squeezed her hand before they walked into the museum.

"See you at happy hour," he said quietly as they went their separate ways.

Veronica tried to not to check the clock constantly as happy hour inched closer. When it was finally the end of the day, she powered down her computer, shut the lights in her office and made her way to Classroom B.

She immediately saw someone at happy hour who rarely made appearances. After grabbing a drink, Veronica made her way to Pilar and started chatting with her.

"What are you doing here? You never come to happy hour," Veronica asked, pleased to see her volunteer outside of the botany collection.

"The drive home after the Behind-the-Scenes event this week wasn't so bad, so I thought why not stick around for happy hour for once," Pilar explained, smiling back at Veronica.

They discussed the Behind-the-Scenes event, noting what worked well and what improvements they might already want to plan for the next year. They were just starting to brainstorm about what they'd like to focus on next time, when a familiar warmth approached Veronica's side.

Artie offered a quiet hello to both of them, attempting to politely interrupt the conversation.

"Artie, this is Pilar, one of the botany volunteers," Veronica introduced them, realizing they had never met before.

"Pleasure. You must work closely with Veronica. I'm surprised I haven't met you yet," Artie said, shaking her hand.

"I don't come to happy hour often. I live in the south suburbs, so it's a long commute," Pilar replied with a hint of shame.

"Pilar was my first volunteer," Veronica gleamed. "I couldn't have grown our database without her help and all of the hours she puts in."

Pilar smiled back at Veronica, soaking up the praise.

"So how did you start working in the Division of Botany?" Artie asked. Veronica noticed that he didn't leave it just as "Pleasure," when meeting someone new at happy hour this time. He was engaging in conversation with Pilar. Because she was important to Veronica? Because he was finally feeling a sense of belonging?

"I'm a museum studies major and I was hoping to get some hands-on experience while in undergrad. You know, getting a taste for all aspects of the museum before I determine what I want my focus to be," Pilar explained.

"The thing about Pilar that really brought everything for our digitization together are her photography skills. My goal for digitizing the botany collection initially only included specimen data, not images." Veronica boasted.

"Photography? What kind of photos? Besides plants, of course," Artie joked.

"Of course," Pilar laughed, before continuing, "Portraits are my favorite, but having a basic understanding of how to use a DSLR camera came in handy for the project."

"The project would be a basic inventory if not for her. The images of the specimens really made it that much more accessible to scientists across the globe." Veronica explained.

"All right, boss. I'm going to have to remember this when it comes time for a full-time position." Pilar quipped, making Veronica laugh.

"You know I'd keep you forever if I could, but botany isn't your passion like it is mine," she replied.

"No, I'm still figuring out what part of the museum I want to end up in. I've enjoyed the botany collection, got to dabble in some museum programming, but I'm still figuring out what's next," Pilar sighed.

"Have you worked in the Anthropology collection at all?" Artie asked.

Veronica eyed Artie, curious where he was going with that.

"No, I haven't. Repatriation is something I'd be interested in pursuing eventually, so working in the Anthropology collection has crossed my mind," Pilar said.

Veronica felt a small bit of hope in her chest, and yet her initial reaction was to stifle it, knowing how protective Henry was of the collection.

"When is the next time you're volunteering? If I'm here, I can show you around the collection area," he offered. Veronica looked to him, scanning his eyes, trying to determine if he knew he might be getting her hopes up.

Artie put a hand in his pocket and held Veronica's eye contact. All she could do was hope it was a reassuring look.

"I'd love that," Pilar and Artie made plans for the next time she'd be onsite, before she ended her evening with, "I've got to head out, bit of a drive ahead of me."

"I'll walk with you to the parking garage," Veronica glanced at Artie, to gauge if this was goodbye for them, too. It had become a habit, him driving her to the train station on Fridays after happy hour.

"I'm parked there too, I'll call it a day," Artie confirmed. Veronica hoped that he too had started to look forward to their weekly routine.

They said goodbye to Pilar near her car, and Veronica deliberately didn't approach Artie's car until Pilar had driven away. Artie noticed, and slowed his pace as he unlocked his vehicle, waiting for Veronica to catch up. Once she let herself into his car, they exchanged knowing looks, the secret between them needing no explanation.

As they drove toward the train station, Artie put his hand on her thigh and gently squeezed, reassuringly. Veronica smiled to herself, looking out the passenger window at the city blocks passing by. Hiding her grin from Artie, hiding how much she enjoyed his touch and how he seemed to be constantly touching her in the moments they found themselves alone.

Mindlessly, his hand seemed to find its way to the back of her neck, his fingers rhythmically stroking her there, sending chills down her body. For someone that has an aggressive side, all Veronica felt in this moment was tenderness from him.

"How was your week?" Veronica asked to displace the buzzing in her head from his touch. She felt like she hadn't seen him much that week outside of their walk along the lake.

"I actually had a first round of interviews with the nearby private university as a postdoc researcher in their anthropology lab. How about you, how was your week?"

Veronica ignored his question at the end, focusing on his news of an interview. "Postdoc researcher in a lab?"

Artie side-eyed her as he explained, "I didn't think much of it. I wasn't sure if I wanted to pursue a career in academia. I'm invited back to do another interview, which is scheduled for next week."

"They must have liked you if they invited you back for another interview. Did you like them?"

Artie's tone was suddenly serious, "Veronica, I loved being on campus. The buildings are all gothic architecture, the stuff old poets dream about."

She beamed, "Artie, that is so exciting."

Artie parked the car, and grabbed Veronica's hand to kiss it before he stepped out to meet her on the passenger side.

Once on the sidewalk, the car still running beside them, Artie tucked a stray wave of hair behind her ear and kept his hand next to her chin.

"I'll see you tomorrow," she said, her chin pointing up to him. She relished in his touch, and the comfort of knowing she'd be seeing him again so soon. Despite the constant worry she had from her past relationships, Artie was starting to feel safe, reliable, and like someone she could count on.

"Tomorrow can't come soon enough."

Chapter 23

The next morning, Veronica did her best to enjoy a quiet morning to herself with a cup of coffee. She busied herself by tidying up her apartment that she had neglected all week due to the longer days she worked for the Behind-the-Scenes event. It was an attempt to not dwell on the evening before her. She told herself it was just dinner. Dinner with Artie, and his family.

In the middle of moving extra shoes and jackets that had piled up in the living room back to her closet, her phone was nearby, and it let out a familiar ding.

ARTIE: *Nothing, just yourself.*

That was his response to Veronica asking what she should bring to his parents' house that evening. And it wasn't helpful at all. Her mind oscillated between flowers, wine, and chocolates - the usual kinds of items someone would bring to a stranger's house. She didn't know them well enough to know if they liked chocolate, or if they were drinkers.

VERONICA: *Not helpful!*

ARTIE: *I'm bringing something from both of us.*

She felt a little at ease knowing that they wouldn't be showing up empty-handed, but also felt the need to bring something from herself. She could practically hear her own mother's disappointment if she didn't. And with the thought of her mom, the woman who constantly had a vase full of fresh flowers at home, Veronica decided flowers would be something generic enough, while personal at the same time since it had meaning to her and her family.

Veronica walked down the block to the closest shop that sold fresh flowers and asked for the bouquet to be wrapped in brown paper, like her mom always did when collecting from the backyard. The paper made unwrapping the blooms more like an experience, exposing the petals only after their fragrance filled the room. Clear plastic wrapped flowers felt dull in comparison. Brown paper packages always felt more like a present.

Artie texted to ask for her address, and that he was on his way to pick her up. After waiting a little while inside her apartment, Veronica grabbed her bag and the fresh flowers and headed downstairs to wait outside, her nerves needing something to do besides stare at the walls of her living room. She sat on the bench at the top of her stoop, watching the cars drive east on the one-way street.

Artie pulled up, parked his car, and got out to greet her, instead of waiting in the car for her to enter.

"Well, now I can assure you that the train station I've been dropping you off at is not out of my way, and neither is your apartment," Artie said, walking to her gate.

"Oh?" Veronica said, stepping down the porch stairs toward him, "I guess which train I was getting on never came up."

"I live on the west side too, but further west, which is why I drive," he shared, meeting her right when she unlatched the iron gate in front of her building.

"So, it was a quick drive?" she asked.

"Very quick," was all he said, when his eyes fell onto the paper wrapped bouquet in her arms. "I said you didn't have to bring anything."

"I couldn't come empty-handed, it's the first time I'm meeting your family."

He smiled, his eyes were no longer on the flowers and instead were on Veronica's face. He looked down at her lips, and it was all Veronica needed as permission to lean closer to him, meeting his kiss halfway. For the moment that they kissed, she let herself get lost in it, until she had to grab the fence at her side to steady herself and pull away.

"What flowers does a botanist choose to bring for an occasion like this?" he said, his voice close and low.

"Peonies. They're in season and bloom for such a short amount of time." Veronica shared, leaning the bouquet toward Artie for him to catch a glimpse at the round, pink bulbs, barely peeking open.

Artie looked at the bouquet, smiling, and then back at his car, "Let's go." He opened the car door for her, letting her in and following into his own seat shortly behind her.

"You told me your moms cooking is good, what else should I know? Any siblings?" Veronica asked, once they were on the road.

"A little sister, and a few of my cousins live in the city too. I have even more cousins in Brazil if you can believe it." he replied.

"I have a little sister too, Melinda. What's your sister's name?"

"Helena."

"And your parents' names? I'm sure I can't walk in there calling your mom 'Mãe,'" Veronica tried her best to pronounce the accent like Artie did.

Laughing, he shared, "My mãe is Carolina, and my pai is João." His accent was thick, especially on their names.

"Carolina and João," Veronica repeated, trying her best to pronounce their names the same way.

"You're doing great," he encouraged. His hand reached over to squeeze her thigh closest to him since her hands were busy holding the flowers, playing mindlessly with the paper.

A short drive later, they pulled up to a bungalow home that was covered in bricks, mirroring all of the other brick homes on the block. Artie parked and met Veronica on her side of the car to walk together. He was holding a bottle of something.

"What's this?" she asked.

"Cachaça, to make some drinks. I can make you one."

Artie didn't knock on the door, and didn't even hesitate as he let himself in and called out to his parents. The first person to appear was a woman with dark hair and honey eyes, Artie's eyes, which Veronica assumed to be his mom. She exclaimed some things in Portuguese and embraced Artie, before she pulled Veronica in for a hug too, already feeling familial.

"You never bring anything!" Artie's mom exclaimed as she held the bottle of clear liquor up, incredulous. Besides the dark hair and the eyes, Veronica didn't see much resemblance in Artie and his mom.

"It's from both of us," he reassured.

"And flowers - from a botanist. How beautiful, thank you," Carolina remarked as she took the flowers that Veronica offered, and spun into the kitchen to grab a vase for the bouquet and to put the cachaça on the corner of the kitchen counter with the other beverages. Veronica felt warm and fuzzy realizing that he must have told his mom that she was a botanist, and that she remembered. "Artie, get yourselves something to drink and head out back."

Veronica followed Artie like a shadow, unsure what to do as she was still getting comfortable. Thankfully, he decided to make cocktails and talked her through it to fill the silence while his mother prepared some dishes in the kitchen.

"Have you ever had a caipirinha?" Artie asked.

"No, but I've heard of it. Is it like a mojito?" she questioned.

"Kind of, but no mint. And better." Artie grabbed the ingredients all laid out in front of him and two glasses. "It's just sugar and lime juice, muddled together. Topped with ice, and cachaça. The other ingredient is time."

"Time?" Veronica questioned.

"It needs to sit for a few minutes, the flavors need time to come together. This way," Artie grabbed their drinks and led Veronica past the kitchen to introduce her to the rest of the family.

The door squeaked as they went out back, and immediately Veronica eased with the sound of Brazilian music and the cacophony of many conversations taking place all at once at various volumes. It was a spring day with some clouds and humidity that threatened rain, but the sun peeked out, warming everyone's skin. The cloud cover offered a coolness that offset Veronica's nerves that would otherwise be making her nervously sweat.

Artie introduced her to his family members; João, Helena, and his aunts, uncles, and cousins were all in the backyard. João pulled Veronica into a hug just like Carolina did. Veronica could see that while Artie had his mom's eyes, everything else about him looked like his dad, but a younger version.

When she was introduced to his sister, Helena, she could see now that she was a spitting image of her mom, but perhaps two decades in the past and with long hair skimming the middle of her back. And it made sense why, when Veronica spotted them together at the old movie theater, she didn't put together that they were siblings. Artie's looks favored their father's side of the family, and Helena's features were more akin to their mother's.

"Is there a special occasion this weekend?" Veronica asked Artie, taking in that so many family members came together for food, music, and drinks.

"No, why?" Artie asked.

"It just seems like so much for just a get-together with family," Veronica remarked.

Artie let out a laugh, "You should see my aunt and uncle's anniversary party each year. Every five years they get a band," he replied with a smile.

People were congregating throughout little sections of the backyard, some in mismatched chairs in the shade of an oak tree, and some by the grill, the smoke from the fire blending into the cloudy sky above them.

Veronica followed Artie to a seat among various family members, and she could hear a combination of some people speaking Portuguese with each other, and some people speaking English.

Carolina brought platters of food outside and spread them across the tables, then motioned to everyone to eat. Veronica's eyes scanned the table, trying to decipher what was on the menu for the night.

Artie's family started making their way to grab plates and serve themselves, not shy. Artie saw Veronica taking it all in, so he leaned close and explained, "That's feijoada, which is essentially beans and meat, and you can serve it with rice. That's picanha, a really tender meat, and there's yuca, kind of like a potato, and collard greens that my aunt made."

"Everything smells good. I'll just have what you're having," she said as she followed him to make a plate for herself. As they made an informal line, Artie's sister found herself behind Veronica.

"Do you like chocolate?" Helena asked, pointing to a platter of little chocolate balls enveloped in chocolate sprinkles.

"Of course, I do," Veronica replied, "Chocolate is a tree."

Helena laughed and nodded her head to her, "Then you'll like these. They're made with chocolate and caramel, and sprinkles. Pretty easy to make actually."

"Chocolate is a tree," Artie said, looking at her sideways, "I like that." Veronica could see the thoughts turning over in his head. Perhaps that was the poetic part of his brain stringing words together.

Artie and Veronica each took a brigadeiro and made their way to sit and eat with the rest of the family. Veronica happily tried all of the food and could see how everything could be comfort food for Artie: warm and soothing and familiar. When she took a bite of the brigadeiro, the chocolate melted in her mouth and she began salivating for more.

"Wow. These are so tasty. Artie, you said your moms cooking was good, but I think you meant great. Everything was so delicious. Maybe it's because I don't get to visit my parents often and have a feast cooked by my mom regularly, but this was missing from my life." Veronica said, eyeing the table with all the food for a second serving.

"I'm glad you like it as much as I do. You should tell my mom," Artie told her.

"Tell me what?" as if on command, Carolina appeared with a plate of her own, the last one to sit down and eat.

"Veronica was saying the food is really good," he repeated.

"I said great. Delicious. Really, I'm feeling a bit spoiled." Veronica clarified.

"Don't be silly, this is what we do," Carolina waved away the compliment like it was nothing.

Artie's sister was listening in on the conversation, and eating her own brigadeiro when she asked, "So, how did you two meet?"

Veronica wasn't sure if Artie had told his family the truth about meeting at work, which she still felt a little uncomfortable with.

"The museum happy hour," Artie replied quickly and succinctly. Veronica noted that he did tell the truth and didn't try to hide the working relationship.

"I'm in the Division of Botany, on staff. And with Artie being a fellow in Anthropology, we don't often cross paths. Except at the happy hour," Veronica added, feeling the need to clarify that they weren't directly working together.

"I'm glad I got the fellowship," Artie said to no one in particular, but he reached his hand over to hers and kissed the back of it, simultaneously reassuring her, and claiming her in front of his family.

"I'm not surprised you got the fellowship, with your confidence," Helena said to her brother.

"Confidence? I thought Artie was kind of quiet the first few times we interacted," Veronica offered.

"He has the 'thinks he knows best' older brother vibe going. Growing up in this family, the oldest boy can do no wrong, and is always right," Helena replied. She narrowed her eyes but smiled at the same time. Veronica could sense the teasing between the two siblings.

"Listen, I mean this in the most respectful way, but don't listen to a word my sister says," Artie joked to Veronica. She laughed along with the siblings. He continued, "I can turn on the confidence for a job interview. But like many, I am also a victim of people-pleasing as a defense mechanism, I want people to like me. It can be both."

Helena nodded with a small smile but didn't ask any follow-up questions. She seemed quiet, like Artie could be before he warmed up to people. Veronica felt herself eager to gain her approval.

After the plates were cleared, Artie and Veronica helped carry the nearly empty platters of food back inside with his aunts and cousins. They returned to their drinks outside, and the last of the day's light turned the backyard orange.

"When you're ready to leave, just let me know," Artie whispered into her neck as he rubbed her back, his lips close to her skin and his breath warm.

"This is your family gathering, we can stay as long as you usually do," she replied, being polite.

Artie pulled back, his eyes finding hers, "Veronica, this is a Brazilian family. They will stay all night."

Veronica laughed, "You're joking."

"I assure you I am not. We can leave at any time, just say the word."

But Veronica didn't have to say anything. Half an hour later, her belly full of picanha and brigadeiro, and her last caipirinha nearly empty, she yawned and tried to hide it.

Artie spotted the irregular intake of breath, and took that as a cue, without having to be told. He stood up, and announced, "We're heading out."

It took another fifteen minutes of goodbyes and hugs and leftovers put into plastic containers for Artie before they were truly ready to go. The rest of the family returned to the backyard, leaving Artie and Veronica in the house, alone. Steps from the front door, she peered down the hallway.

"Is this where you grew up?" she asked quietly.

Artie nodded quietly and his eyes followed her gaze down the hall, "Why? Do you want to see my room?" Artie gave her a look, both mischievous and yearning. Veronica nodded, too.

Without a word he took her hand and led her down the dim hall toward a closed door. When he opened it, he flicked the light switch on and only a small bedside lamp illuminated the space. The room was a mix of what Veronica suspected were remnants from his teenage boy era, and more recently his mom's empty nest era. There were posters tacked onto the walls of Brazilian soccer players, and a desk in the corner with a sewing machine and a pile of projects next to it.

"Big soccer fan?" Veronica confirmed, as she walked around the room, her eyes taking in the details.

"Football, technically." Artie stood back at the doorway, leaning on the frame as he watched her look around.

"Big fan of sewing, too?" she teased.

Artie smiled before he played along, "It's one of the oldest textile arts. So, naturally, as an anthropologist, it's in my benefit to get into it."

Artie dipped his chin as he watched her. Veronica wasn't looking for anything in particular, it was simply her curiosity that led her to ask about his room.

"What was little Artie like?" she asked, her eyes scanning the abandoned toys and knick-knacks that lined the top of his dresser and the old desk in the corner.

"Well, he was mostly called Arturo then. Quiet among a big, boisterous family."

"Your sister doesn't seem to think you're quiet," Veronica suggested as she sat down on the edge of his childhood bed.

He walked toward her and leaned down, placing his hands on the bed on either side of her hips as he towered over her. He barricaded her in as he whispered into her neck, "Please don't talk about my sister as I enjoy watching the girl of my dreams sit on my childhood bed."

His breath warmed her neck, and she felt herself leaning into it. One heartbeat later, the door to the backyard squeaked, and someone's feet made their way down the hall to the bathroom.

Artie quickly stood up and turned the light switch off.

Veronica stood, laughing, "You think us in here with the lights off is going to make this anymore inconspicuous?"

"I have a girl in my room, in my parents' house, forgive me if I'm a little on edge," Artie said in the dark.

Veronica enjoyed seeing this side of Artie, a little vulnerable. She ached to peel back more and more of his layers. She let herself give in to the desire. "Then show me your room, in your place," she requested, and his only response was a nod.

Veronica silently walked toward him in the dark and opened his bedroom door for them to leave. They made their way out the front door and quietly into his car. The evening light was just about disappearing, and the sugar from Veronica's caipirinha was catching up to her, giving her a second wind.

"Your family is so nice. Really, everyone was so welcoming," she shared, her ear leaning on the headrest as she looked toward Artie as her turned the key in the car's ignition.

"Thanks for listening to my father's stories. I know his accent can be hard to understand," Artie said, glimpsing over to her.

She beamed, "His stories were great, don't apologize. Only hard to follow sometimes, but I caught on to the key points." She paused, waiting for Artie to reply, but no response came. Instead, he sat quietly in the driver's seat, so she continued, "People like your parents, your aunts and uncles and cousins, and *you* make this city alive. That's why cities are great, you can have Japanese pub food one night, and the world's best caipirinha the next. That's why I wanted to move to the city. To be surrounded with this variety. I know you might not feel it, but you do belong here. The city is a city because of people like you."

She reached for his hand, holding it, and his eyes went from his lap to her face. She knew he yearned for a sense of belonging, and he ate up her words.

He leaned over toward her and claimed her mouth with his. She let go of his hands and he moved his fingers into her hair, wide and searching. His kiss moved from her mouth, down her neck.

Artie kissed her lips one more time, before slamming his seatbelt into place. He drove toward the downtown skyline in the distance, making their way back, closer to the city. Veronica felt the electricity between them, their kiss being cut short. Artie must have felt it too, and he rested his hand on her thigh closest to him. The closer they got to his apartment, the closer his hand inched up her leg.

Artie pulled off the main road into a neighborhood with many trees, the night instantly feeling later with the darkness under the large branches. They drove past old houses with charm, each one different from the next. He finally pulled into the driveway of a large house and parked all the way at the end.

Veronica's eyes stared up at the immense home on the other side of her window. She had many questions, having just come from a modest family home, and now sitting in the driveway of what could be a historic home.

"I don't live in that house," Artie clarified, noting the confused look on her face. "I rent the guest house."

Veronica followed his finger that pointed to the small cottage at the corner of the property. That made more sense for a postdoc.

She followed him to the door, an old wooden one that matched the style of the larger home on the property. When he opened it, Veronica saw one room that encompassed a sitting area with an old fireplace and a small, round table in the corner for meals. The kitchen was right there too, open to the entire space, neat and updated.

Artie flicked on some lights and put his keys down, Veronica caught a glimpse of his routine, the autopilot motions of coming home. "Can I get you something to drink? Wine, beer, water?" he offered.

"Actually, do you have some tea?" she asked.

"I'm not a big tea drinker, but I might have something." He crossed the room to the kitchen and rummaged in a cabinet, pushing aside various bags of coffee, until he located the only box of tea he had. "Yerba mate?" he offered, "It's like green tea."

"Perfect," Veronica smiled politely. She felt unsettled and nervous being in yet another new place. She wasn't sure if she should sit or stand. Instead, she walked around the small perimeter of the sitting area, and looked at the spines of the books there were on the shelves. She found anthropology textbooks, books of poetry, and classic novels. One book stood out to her, its spine the largest one on the shelf.

"Anything interesting?" he asked, placing two cups of tea down on the coffee table.

She held up the large book of quotations and remarked "This is massive."

"It's a book of quotations. I find it helpful when I need to be a bit inspired. For poetry," he said, already sipping his steaming cup of tea.

Veronica brought it over to the coffee table to look through it as they sipped from their mugs.

"I had fun today," Artie said, looking over at her, catching her eyes and holding her gaze before adding, "With you."

"Me too," she replied, and meant it. She warmed her hands with her mug of tea, cupping it in her hands to transfer the heat. As she waited for the tea to warm her from the inside and out, her eyes skimmed the book of quotations, but she couldn't focus on any of the words. Instead, she asked, "You speak Portuguese, right?"

"Yeah," Artie replied, "Remember, saudades?"

"Yeah, I remember," Veronica said. She paused as she remembered the few words that he had taught her. "It's just that... you weren't speaking it with your parents or cousins or aunts and uncles."

He glanced off into the distance for a moment before he answered, "I speak Portuguese, but I feel almost like an imposter. My accent isn't like theirs. I'm more comfortable in English at this point. I feels like I'm putting on an act when I speak it. It doesn't feel natural. Though I wish it did."

She didn't know what to say. But she was glad that he had shared, so she simply put one of her hands on his.

Veronica felt the emptiness of the space between them. With so much of their time spent together at the museum where they couldn't be close, she wanted to take advantage of every moment outside of the museum together that she could.

She put her tea mug back on the coffee table and inched closer to him. Artie brushed her dark waves off her shoulder, holding his hand next to her hair for a long beat before he leaned in and brought her face to meet his.

They stayed kissing on the couch for some time, and Veronica waited for Artie to make the next move. Suddenly, he stood up and he lifted his shirt up over his head, freeing his torso. In the light of his living room, for the first time Veronica noticed the freckles that spotted his shoulders and faded into a sea of caramel below his biceps. Artie reached out his hand and invited her to his bedroom.

The next morning, a sliver of sunlight was spotlighting the art on the wall. Veronica opened her eyes to the intense light, focusing on the art while she registered where she was. In Artie's bedroom, in Artie's bed, she stirred.

"Let me make some coffee," he said, his voice husky with sleep. He stirred now that she was finally awake too.

They both got out of the bed, and when Veronica went to put on her clothes from the day before, Artie offered, "Do you want something clean to wear?"

"What do you have in mind?" she questioned.

Artie crossed the room to a dresser drawer, his feet soft on the floor, taking out a t-shirt with the name of a local ice cream shop on it, and a pair of soccer shorts, and handed them to her.

They both got dressed silently, and took turns in the bathroom, freshening up. When Veronica came out to the smell of coffee, Artie asked, "What do you typically eat for breakfast?"

"I'll eat whatever you're making."

Artie opened his fridge, scanning his inventory. "I can probably make a standard American breakfast, eggs and toast. Or I can make a standard Brazilian breakfast, which is fruit and sandwiches, if you can believe it."

"Is your cooking as good as your moms?" Veronica teased.

"Definitely not," he deadpanned. "Maybe let's stick to the one that doesn't actually require any cooking."

"Your Brazilian breakfast? I'm in."

"Coffee?" he offered, holding an empty mug.

"Yes, please."

Artie made his way around the kitchen, starting with filling her mug with coffee, which gave Veronica something to hold onto while he prepped everything else.

"How do you take your coffee?"

"Lots of milk, like latte levels of milk. And the steamier the better."

He laughed, reaching for the milk to pour into her mug. "I've never had someone describe coffee almost inappropriately."

"How would you describe your coffee then?"

"I also like it hot," he takes a slow sip of his own mug, maintaining eye contact.

After a moment, he plated some brioche-like rolls with slices of meat and cheese for little breakfast sandwiches. He sliced up some fruit on another plate, taking his time with the mango, peeling it. His knife rocked effortlessly on the cutting board, the blade and his hand were the only things that moved, rhythmically back and forth.

"Sorry I'm not more prepared to cook. I'll cook dinner for you sometime, I promise." Artie said. He brought their two plates of food to the small, round table in the corner for them to eat.

"This is great. The mango is perfectly ripe," she admired, as she took a seat and started eating.

"Mangoes always remind me of Brazil. I've never had a mango here that tastes as good as they do there," he said, his eyes glossing over almost as if he was transported back there for a moment.

"Well, this one tastes pretty perfect to me," she leaned over to kiss him, tasting the sweetness of fruit on both of their lips.

"I've got soccer today, but you can stay as long as you like," he offered when breakfast came to an end.

"Thanks, but I'll head home," she said, standing to clear the table. "And thanks for coffee, and breakfast, and for inviting me over last night."

He smiled, rising to meet her, "Thank you for last night."

Artie's plans for his day sparked her to ask, "If you have soccer today, does that mean you'll need your shorts back?"

He glanced down at her hips, "As much as I'd love for you to take them off, keep 'em. I've got others."

As he continued getting ready for soccer practice, he reached for a reusable water bottle to fill. He pushed it against the door of the refrigerator, the water filter clicking as the bottle began to fill. While Artie waited for it to fill, he gave her a look, a longing one, and Veronica couldn't help but make her way closer. His head tilted to the side slightly, his eyes moving from hers down to her lips, inviting her to kiss. And that was the last thing she saw until she closed her eyes and kissed him. Their lips touched and each of their mouths instantly parted, their tongues finding each other. The kiss was slow, and lazy: the perfect Sunday morning kiss. Until Veronica heard Artie stop and say, "Oh my god," as he pulled away. She felt the water splash to her feet before she saw it. They both looked at his hand and the water that had overflowed down the refrigerator door.

Artie pulled the bottle of water away from the refrigerator, the flow stopping with a thunk.

"Oh," was all she said, realizing their kiss took them away to a place that wasn't here, a place where Artie forgot he was filling a bottle with water. She felt an ache in her pelvic, hungry for another kiss, hungry for the place the kiss just took them.

Artie put the full bottle on the counter and reached for a towel to soak up the mess.

"Sorry," she said quietly, almost embarrassed.

"Don't be," he replied, his expression going from longing to cheeky.

Once he wiped up the floor, they kissed again, and Artie sighed, reluctantly, "I'll drive you home."

Chapter 24

It was the first nice day of the season. The rain clouds seemed to be behind them, not a lick of humidity in the air. The sun was shining, but a cool spring breeze made the sun's warmth barely touch the skin. Veronica decided it was the perfect day to start biking to work for the season.

The museum sat on the edge of a lake, with the perfect pedestrian and bike path leading from her apartment to museum campus. Even on the warmest days, the lake's wind made the bike ride irresistible. On her bike, the city's wind rushed against her cheeks, and her hair whipped and tickled her neck as it danced. The movement was a constant reminder that she was alive, actively getting from point A to point B.

Veronica arrived at work warm, but not sweaty, with hair that was matted at the top from her helmet, yet tousled at the ends from the wind, and still a little damp from her shower that morning. She pushed her steel frame bike through the loading dock entrance of the museum and locked it up. Then, she spent a few minutes in the restroom, touching up her hair before heading to her office.

The calendar alert for the monthly staff meeting went off almost as soon as Veronica sat down at her desk. Gathering a notebook and a pen, she made her way to the museum's lecture hall to find a spot.

Just outside of the lecture hall, dozens of the museum's staff members were milling about. There were tables setup with quick service breakfast items like bagels and bananas, but Veronica headed right for the coffee table.

Among a sea of staff members holding cups of coffee, she recognized the torso of a tall man, reaching down to pour himself a cup, so she sidled up to the familiar individual.

"Hey, Artie," she said, pouring herself a cup of hot coffee from the dispenser.

"Hey," he replied, standing up to his full height with his own cup, covering the black coffee with a lid.

Veronica glanced at his drink, as she awkwardly danced with another staff member that was reaching around her for the oat milk.

"That answers that question," she teased, her eyes darting from the coffee in his hands to his confused expression.

"What?" he said, looking down at himself self-consciously.

"How you take your coffee."

"Was it a question?"

"I didn't notice yesterday. But now I know how you like your coffee in the mornings."

They shared a smile with each other, soaking in their shared secret, with their unmistakable chemistry. They moved out of the way for others to grab a cup.

Artie sipped his coffee, making a face.

"What's that face?" she asked.

"This tastes a bit too weak for me. This coffee is the kind you can see through. I prefer the kind you can skate on top of."

Veronica let out a laugh, feeling like she was swimming in warm fuzzies. Artie, the comedian, the poet, the fox.

"Can I sit with you?" he asked, quieter this time.

"Of course. I thought at this point it was a given," she alluded.

"I didn't want to assume," Artie trailed off, leaning closer to her with a hushed voice, "In case you didn't want to draw attention to this, to us, to whatever -"

Artie stammered, and Veronica calmly placed a hand on his forearm that held his coffee. "I'm not worried."

As quickly as she placed her hand on his arm, she drew it away. But his arm still tingled where her skin had been briefly.

Veronica and Artie took their seats at the staff meeting. Pilar walked down their row of chairs, sat next to Veronica and offered a quiet wave hello to Artie.

The meeting started standard enough, with the museum president discussing the museum's mission - sharing science. The future of the museum was discussed, and notably, Veronica's ears perked up when she heard the president start to discuss accessibility.

"Museum collections can feel dated. Even the way collections used to be acquired is an archaic method. We can't fall prey to doing things the way it's always been done..." the president was saying, but then Veronica's attention was interrupted.

"Acquired? More like taken," Pilar quietly quipped in her seat.

"Making the museum's most valuable collections available to all, both scientists and visitors alike. Even to those who cannot physically visit our halls, that is an important aspect of our mission, and our future. As we approach the halfway mark of this year, I'd like everyone to start thinking about how we can pursue that goal, physically. Ideally attainable goals can be mapped out for each department to start achieving accessibility next year."

Pilar was nodding in agreement next to Veronica. Veronica felt proud that her digitization work was already a step in that direction. And before she could start to even consider ways to expand on it, she thought of Pilar at her side.

And how Pilar was interested in anthropology. And how digitizing that collection would be a step in the direction of the museum's mission - right from the mouth of the president. How could anyone, including Henry, deny that?

Veronica took out her phone to check her calendar for the rest of the day. She wanted to see if she had time to meet with Henry informally to chat through an idea. She confirmed she was free, and scanned the room for a sighting of him. With Artie at her side, and not with Henry, she couldn't just look for one of the tallest heads in the theater seats.

She didn't see him among the crowd, so she figured she would stop by the anthropology lab after the staff meeting.

A few other department heads spoke at the staff meeting, sharing notable updates and celebrating milestones.

Once it ended, Veronica nearly jumped out of her seat and quickly said goodbye to both Pilar and Artie, even though he might have been heading to the same place.

She approached the lab, and knocked gently on the door, and then waved to Henry through the window for him to let her in. Like usual, her staff badge did not give her access to the anthropology collections and lab.

Henry let Veronica in, and the fact that he was already working on something in the lab made her wonder if he had left the staff meeting early. Or maybe he wasn't there at all. She took a seat next to Henry, and they exchanged hellos and quick small talk, before Veronica dove in.

"Remember when we briefly discussed digitizing the anthropological collections?" she asked, attempting to keep her expectations low.

"Yes, I remember. Unfortunately, we still don't have the resources to allocate staff to digitization," Henry replied, his voice stale.

"I know you've said Anthropology has never had volunteers before due to the sensitive nature of the collection, but I have a volunteer. She's not just any volunteer; her name is Pilar. She has been volunteering with me since I began our digitization efforts," Veronica explained. She thought she could see Henry's reluctance fading, his wall coming down. She felt a bit more confident and continued, "She's reliable, trustworthy, and absolutely dedicated to sharing our collections and our scientific research. I think she would make a great asset to your department."

"I trust that she is, but there are no plans to start a volunteer program in Anthropology at this time," Henry said.

Veronica sighed involuntarily. She didn't want to give up, she thought she almost had him.

"I really was hoping you'd reconsider with Pilar potentially leading the effort. We just had the staff meeting, and our president really pressed the importance of the museum's mission, sharing science, making the collections more accessible. Especially collections as valuable as Anthropology," Veronica tried flattery, a different angle to attempt to warm him to the idea.

His facial expression hadn't changed. He was slowly breathing in, but still, wordless.

"I think this would be a really great way to support the initiative," Veronica gave it one last shot, still brimming with hope.

"Sorry, no."

That was it. That was all he said, and then he slightly turned his back toward her, letting her know that the conversation was over.

Veronica sat back, really giving up this time. Hope left her and was replaced with anger. She felt that this was completely against the museum mission and didn't align with the president's hope to highlight some of the most valued collections. She felt that he wasn't really listening to her. She was helpless to persuade him, and the lack of control to pursue the mission of a museum that was incredibly important to her.

Feeling defeated, Veronica offered a quiet and curt goodbye, and left the Anthropology lab.

Veronica walked out of the lab and let the door close behind her, but she didn't hear the footsteps on the limestone floor behind her. She didn't even hear the echoes of museums guests murmuring through the halls outside of the lab. Instead, she only heard her own thoughts, until a familiar voice called out.

"Veronica, wait," Artie's voice called after her as he caught up and fell into step with her.

Veronica didn't know what to say, her mind was still going through the conversation she just had, still feeling defeat. She found herself walking toward the museum exit instead of back to her office.

"I'm going for a walk along the lake," she said quietly to Artie.

"I know how he seems," he replied.

"You mean how he doesn't even give anyone else's ideas a chance? Are you condoning his sense of superiority?" Veronica asked. Her anger came out in her voice, and as she slammed the exit door handles outward. She stepped into the cool air coming off the lake and felt tears stinging her eyes as she left the museum in her wake.

"No, but I understand where he's coming from. There's a reason why he's so protective of the collection that he oversees. There's a reason why he is the way he is." Artie explained.

"That doesn't make his behavior okay," Veronica replied, annoyed, before he could even continue. She didn't want to hear any more excuses, "He doesn't even listen to me, doesn't give me a chance. He can't go through life dismissing other people's ideas because he wants to keep his collection all to himself and traditional anthropologists. A museum would be nothing without its collection, and we as staff are a collective of some of the greatest scientists working together. Except him, he refuses to work with anyone."

Veronica huffed as they walked together, frustrated with the idea of a part of the museum not being accessible to all, let alone a volunteer who has already proven themselves trustworthy of the museum's collection. She was annoyed and felt the heat in her chest boil into bitterness. She stopped walking for a moment and took a deep breath to keep her anger and her tears at bay.

"Don't let him," Artie pleaded, his eyes locked on hers. One thing she adored about him was his great ability to hold eye contact, and to make her feel like she was the most important thing in the world when he did.

"Don't let him do what?" Veronica asked softly as she stood at the edge of the lakefront path and held his gaze.

"Don't let Henry get to you," he said plainly.

"Artie, this isn't about Henry, this is about doing what is best for the museum. How can you not advocate for that?" She felt like she was nearly begging him to understand her perspective.

"I'm just a visiting researcher, here for a season, and then moving on. I have no skin in the game," Artie raised his voice, exasperated. "But I'm just trying to be here for you. I can tell you're upset."

Veronica bit the inside of her cheek to keep herself from saying anything sharp. She thought that if he didn't fight for it, if he wasn't passionate about right versus wrong, about the mission of the museum's collection, then she felt they weren't as similar as she thought.

She breathed in and out slowly, regulating her irritability with her breath, and steadily continued, "But you can still make a difference. Change the way we do things for the better. You can have a positive impact and advocate for a great initiative that benefits the museum's mission. Henry might listen to you. He might actually listen if more people advocate for this. Don't let your time here be wasted."

Artie looked at her blankly, "Does everything have to benefit your definition of being worthwhile? Let it go."

Veronica felt the cold words cut through her. She thought back to what his sister teased him for: older brother, always right. *Did he really not understand? Was he really not going to fight for this?* she thought. *And was he really capable of saying something that unkind?*

Through her quiet pause, Artie kept going, "My fellowship is based on set parameters of research. The end goal is not to contribute to the museum mission, it's not to persuade Henry to change his behavior, and it's not to ensure that it's not wasted — something you are so focused on. My research just might be as simple as that, just research. Nothing more and nothing less." He paused, and she was still quiet, letting his words sink in. He took a step back, and finally continued, "I hate to break it to you, but I'm pretty average. Pretty unspectacular. Not living an extraordinary life that makes a difference, that changes the world, that benefits the greater good - which seems so important to you."

At that moment, Veronica couldn't believe his words. She felt doubt that they could truly be together, sensing that they didn't see eye to eye and that their values didn't align.

There was silence between them for what felt like ages.

Veronica wordlessly thought of what she found more important - her work authenticity? Her love interest? What did she want most moving forward?

In the silence, Artie thought that postdocs already don't have time for relationships. Relationships are not worth the little free time, since more often than not, they don't work out. Just like this.

When the silence became unbearable, Veronica left him on the lakefront and went back inside the museum without him.

Veronica saw the unlabeled specimen before she even got near her office door, sticking out of the mailbox. She quickly grabbed it as she rushed into her office, dashing to her desk like a tornado.

She wanted to cool off; the mysterious unlabeled specimens were the last thing she wanted to deal with at this time. She glanced at the flower. Marigold, a vivid orange and the paper was weighed down with the heaviness of its full bloom.

The label read *Tagetes erecta*. A scientific name like that would normally make Veronica giggle, no matter how old she got. But today, she did not feel like laughing.

She tossed the specimen aside to a pile of papers that she did not need to get to urgently.

Veronica looked around her office, unsure of what to work on next. And yet she knew she wouldn't be able to concentrate on anything.

She considered going to William to ask him what to do, how to advocate for Pilar, for the work she could do and the overall mission of the museum. But she looked at the pile of work on her desk, and the emails in her inbox, and assumed William was also dealing with his own share of work - too busy to advocate for her conflict.

So she didn't go to him.

❀ Part Six ❀

Veronica

Chapter 25

That weekend, Veronica had agreed to visit her family's home for her sister's birthday. Melinda was off celebrating her birthday with friends when Veronica's train arrived at the station, so her mom picked her up instead.

Her mom's old station wagon was just as familiar and comforting to her as walking into her childhood home and seeing her mom's latest vase full of flowers on the kitchen counter.

That afternoon, Melinda came back from her brunch with friends. As a family they ate dinner together, sang happy birthday to the younger sister, and ate cake. Veronica was feeling glad that she could be with her family for celebrations like this, big and small. And yet something about the way they had their own traditions, their own family dynamic, reminded her of the new family that had been recently introduced into her life. Artie's moms cooking brought her comfort, just like her own moms did. The way each family member fell into their own comforting routine, easily finding their place within a home. As Veronica looked around, she found herself wishing she was able to share this moment and her family with someone else that would appreciate it, too. Not just anyone else, but with Artie.

Veronica ended the visit to her family's house as she usually did, curled up on the couch watching cooking and baking shows with her sister. It was a ritual that was simple, and yet warmed her knowing that some things in life she could always count on.

Veronica was only half-watching the baking competition show when her thoughts were interrupted by her sister across the couch.

"What gives?" Melinda asked, nearly invisible under mass amounts of knitted blankets layered on top of her.

"What?" Veronica replied to her sister, her annoyance at being interrupted in thought causing her voice to get higher pitched at the end.

"You've been a bit mopey all weekend, and now you're not even paying attention to the calming, relaxing, cozy vibes of the Great British Bake Off."

Melinda stared at her sister pointedly. She was not wrong, and yet Veronica did not even know where to begin.

How was she supposed to explain that the person she had started getting close to had a fundamentally different view on life? That he didn't have the same goal? Her mind bounced around trying to think of a way to begin explaining the conflict, but instead, she felt that her sister would just echo the fact that they don't see eye to eye, and to just move on.

So, she said nothing.

Melinda dropped Veronica off at the train station the next morning, and Veronica let the roar of the train bring her closer and closer to her home in the city.

A few days later, it was the middle of the week, but Camilla, in true Camilla fashion, invited Veronica out for a drink. Veronica agreed, only if they could go to the dive bar across from her apartment.

Veronica arrived first, naturally, but only had to wait a few minutes before Camilla burst through the door, her energy immediately filling the room.

They cozied up at the bar, surrounded by old photos of Elvis on the walls, colorful Christmas lights strung from the ceiling (year-round), and an unexpected selection of songs playing from the jukebox in the corner.

"How is your new apartment treating you?" Veronica made small talk with her friend, after their drinks had arrived and they were settled.

"It's incredible for the sole fact that I don't have any upstairs neighbor, I *am* the upstairs neighbor. Also, my downstairs neighbor has the cutest dog, rarely barks, and always rolls on his back when I see him. So, you know, an upgrade from the terrible neighbor situation I used to have," Camilla replied, her bracelets clashing together every time she moved, making music with her movements.

"Wow, your neighbor rarely barks and rolls on his back for you? Sounds like a catch. Is he single?" Veronica teased.

Camilla rolled her eyes at her friend. In response, Veronica flashed a smile at her.

"I can only assume that Baby Thor is *not* single, though I have not had any sightings of a significant other," Camilla said nonchalantly.

"Baby Thor?" Veronica asked, but her friend's facial expression did not change. "What makes him a baby? Is he young?"

"No, not young. He looks like Thor, but his hair is shorter. Baby Thor." Camilla clarified.

Veronica nodded along, willing her friend's logic to make sense to her. She was feeling so glad that things were working out better for Camilla. She also envied how secure Camilla was, she was unapologetically herself. Veronica always wanted a little bit of that to rub off her friend and onto her.

After their first round, Camilla excused herself to use the restroom, and while she was gone, Veronica stared absently at the bottles lined up behind the bar.

Her woolgathering was interrupted when a customer came up next to her to order a drink from the bartender. Veronica offered a polite smile and was about to look away, when she noticed the sweater that the man was wearing. It was a university sweatshirt, for the same university that Artie had been interviewing for a postdoc position with.

She wondered how Artie's on campus interview was going. It was supposed to be sometime that week, but because they haven't been talking, she wasn't sure when, what day, if it was multiple days, dinners involved, etc. She wanted to reach out to him to ask, but also felt the rift between them and didn't want to pretend it wasn't there. They needed to talk before they could continue any sort of relationship or friendship.

But who was she kidding, she felt like he might not even want to continue seeing her. Her desire to continue talking to him might be one-sided, and she wasn't ready to find that out. She was still too hurt to put her pride aside and risk finding out if it wasn't only her feeling like he was missing from her.

She considered what she wanted, what felt truest to herself, versus being true to the museum and her work. Or could she give in to her own wishes too and choose to amend things with him?

She realized, with great intensity, how she missed him. She yearned to speak to him again. To make him smile and see his dimples appear. Her body felt like a magnet pulling toward him.

And yet she realized it wasn't that easy. They weren't talking and she was still upset with him. And yet her heart under her rib cage ached to know him again and ached to no longer ache. She wasn't sure if she wished to repair things with him to make the ache go away, or if she wished to no longer care about him at all.

She didn't have to decide that night, nor did she have to dwell on it further because Camilla returned from the restroom, and they continued their catchup session over drinks. Veronica tried to keep her mind off the university, and on her friend in front of her. But more specifically, she tried to keep her mind off Artie.

Chapter 26

William peeked his head into her office, lightly knocking his knuckles on her door as he did. "Are you heading to happy hour?"

It was already another week that had passed, but instinctually Veronica looked at her work calendar to confirm that it was indeed Friday. Her work had wrapped up for the week, but she stared at the slide deck for a webinar that she was a panelist on. The webinar wasn't for another two weeks, but she was getting a jump on it, trying her best to keep her mind busy and distracted with work.

Looking back at William, he gave her an inviting grin. While she didn't feel all that up for going or socializing, part of her wanted to see Artie, even though the other part of her was still upset with him and wanted to avoid him.

"I'll go for just one round," Veronica said to William as she pushed away from her desk.

She arrived at Classroom B and was a little relieved that Artie wasn't there. She felt like she could have typical conversations with her coworkers without tension in the room. But then, as time wore on and he still didn't show, she felt tension growing from the lack of his presence. She couldn't help but start to wonder what it meant.

Was he avoiding her? Avoiding the museum? Did he feel like it was so easy to give up on her? Did he not have the slightest itch to see her again, like she had to see him?

She barely finished her drink when she decided it was time to go. She said goodbye to her colleagues that she was speaking with, and on her way out, a heavy hand gently leaned on her shoulder.

"Heading out?" It was William.

"Yeah, I can only stay for the one," Veronica said sheepishly, tossing her drink into a bin.

"We're low on beer. Help me get a couple of cases before you go?"

He was so earnest, and always kind, Veronica wanted to be kind right back, so she agreed to help him. "Sure."

She followed him out of Classroom B and into the staff elevator to the storage room. Taking the elevator to get more beer reminded her of the last time she helped William at happy hour. It reminded her of the day she had met Artie. And suddenly, she was thinking about his honey-colored eyes, his dimples that framed his bold smile, and his dark waves that fell into his face.

"You seem down," she heard William say, the image of Artie in her mind disappearing as quickly as it came.

"There are some things on my mind."

"Work related?"

"Partly, yes," the elevator stopped, and they walked to the storage area. William unlocked the room and moved aside some cases of beer to grab the crowd favorites.

"If it has anything to do with the museum, I'm all ears. Contrary to popular belief, although you technically report to me, my job is actually to support *you* - in your career goals," William said, as he grabbed a case and handed it to Veronica, then grabbed a case for himself. "And if it has something to do with the museum, but also to do with your personal life, I respect that you may not want to share that with me. But I want you to know that I'm here to support you in your *personal* goals, too."

Veronica looked at him, having the vague feeling as if she was in elementary school, and might be in trouble with the teacher. She wasn't sure what to say, so she said nothing, and they both stood there holding the cases of beer without moving, just looking at each other.

"It's not an HR issue, I assure you. You know how many people in this museum I have seen couple up through the years? You don't work together, I'm not concerned, you are both adults, and it's fine if you decide to keep it private."

Veronica relaxed a little; for one it was no longer a secret she had to keep from her boss, and the second part, to hear that it was not a terrible violation of a workplace policy, also eased her nerves. "That's the thing, it was private and separate, until it wasn't. Frances figured it out pretty quickly once I started hinting at it. Did everyone else realize we were seeing each other?"

"No, just the people who know you really well," he smirked.

"What gave it away?" she asked sheepishly, having the sense that they had been found out a while ago.

"Not just anyone will run across a convention center to make it in time to see a presentation. Especially when it highlights botany, and they are an anthropologist," William said, alluding to the conference. Veronica nodded. "Though I suspected something when he asked me to introduce him to the woman I walked into happy hour with during his first week."

Veronica's eyes went wide, and she felt the smallest heat make its way to her cheeks. She realized the heat wasn't embarrassment from being found out by her boss, but instead were warm fuzzies at the thought of Artie wanting to meet her as soon as he saw her.

She took a breath, getting back to the matter at hand. "The issue we're having is not seeing eye to eye on a museum topic. I'd like to talk to you about one of the volunteers and an opportunity for them to volunteer in Anthropology. I could use your support there."

"Let me go drop off this beer first."

"You mean to talk right now?"

"If you need support, then that's the highest priority item tonight as far as I'm concerned."

Veronica considered, she didn't want to go into it right then, on a Friday evening. It was a long, tiring week. And although she had only had one beer, she had been drinking. "No, I'd rather wait, can we do that?"

"First thing Monday morning then. Come to me when you get into the office, I'll make the time."

"Thanks, William."

"Veronica, this is my job. If there's an opportunity you see for one of the volunteers and you think it will be successful?"

"So successful, for the museum, for science, for various communities -"

William nodded, "I trust your instincts. Let's see what we can do. Monday."

"Thank you," she managed, shifting the case of beer in her arms as the weight got to her.

"Let's offload these now. Thanks for your help," William said, and they made their way back to Classroom B to drop off the beers into the cooler for the rest of the staff that was planning to stay.

Veronica said goodbye to William, and he gave her a reassuring look. She looked around the room one last time, and as she suspected, Artie wasn't there. It occurred to her then, she'd have to walk to the train tonight. It was something she had done many times before, but just like she had looked forward to counting on happy hours with Artie, she realized she had looked forward to their alone time in his car when he'd drop her off at the train station.

She grabbed her bag from her office, turned out the lights, and made her way through the city to her train. She walked toward the station, the last of the evening light dipping behind the skyscrapers, the long shadows of summer stretching across the sidewalks in her path.

Chapter 27

Veronica hadn't heard from Artie all weekend, and likewise, she hadn't reached out to him. The weight of thinking of him, of potentially running into him - now she knew why it wasn't always sanctioned to have workplace romances. A new week began and the gray cloud hung over her as she entered her favorite place in the world, the museum.

She was glad that the botany collections were on the upper floors with the Division of Birds and Division of Insects, while the anthropological collections were underground, in the newer storage areas. The likelihood of an accidental run-in with someone she was glad to avoid was welcomed.

For a brief moment she let herself acknowledge that yes, once again, the Anthropology division gets the VIP treatment with the new collections area, while other divisions remained in the older collections areas with creaky windows, hard to control natural light and temperatures, and a fire-suppression system that was up-to-code, but not state-of-the-art, like anthropology had.

Sighing at the unfairness, she entered her office and was surprised to see someone already there. At first, she assumed William, since it was Monday and the first thing on her list was to go see him. But once the man turned around, the glasses made it obvious that it was Henry.

"How was your weekend?" he asked. It was the first time he had ever asked her a question that wasn't related to the museum.

"Fine, and yours?" Veronica put her things down at her desk but didn't bother to power up her computer.

"Good," was all he said, no follow up questions. "I wanted to talk to you about the volunteer opportunity."

"Okay," Veronica took a breath, not expecting to have that kind of conversation with Henry, before having her conversation with William. Even still, she took a seat at her desk, and motioned for Henry to sit too, at the only other desk and chair in the small room.

He sat and explained, "I wasn't actively listening when you were proposing the idea of a volunteer in Anthropology to digitize the collections. Specifically, Pilar as the volunteer. It's come to my attention that you've developed the botany division's entire volunteer program and digitization efforts. I haven't worked closely with you before, so I didn't realize the scope of your work. I'd like the chance to discuss it again, to consider it for the Anthropology division."

"Did you speak to someone about our volunteer process in botany?" Veronica asked, wondering if William had talked to Henry since their chat at happy hour.

"I think you and I both know that I could talk to anyone in this museum, and they would have only positive things to say about you, your volunteers, and your digitization project. I'm sorry I doubted you. The idea of volunteers in the department is so new, and I'm very protective of the collections, which I'm sure you noticed," he gave a small laugh.

Veronica chuckled to ease the awkward air. "I feel protective of the museum too. I only want to see it and the collections thrive," she added.

"I know, I'm sorry it took so long for me to come around. I'd love to see a formal write up of your digitization process and workflow. And of course, I would love to speak with Pilar if she's still interested."

"I can send you all our documentation. Pilar helped build it, so I really do feel like if there was any particular volunteer that I could trust with sensitive collections, it would be her."

Henry nodded, "Thank you, specifically for understanding the sensitivity of anthropological collections. I realize now, I can't automatically give in to how things are always done. There is always something to learn, to try, and to improve, right? That's what makes us scientists."

Veronica felt like they finally reached some common ground and smiled. "Yes, I can definitely agree with that."

Henry smiled and he stood. "Good, thanks for hearing me out. Again, I'm sorry I wasn't open to it initially. Send me an overview of what you have and connect me with Pilar. I'll prioritize it and schedule a meeting with her right away."

She stood and walked with him to the hallway, "Sounds great. Thanks, Henry. I'm glad we talked."

"Me too," and with that, he waved and headed toward the staff elevator down to the anthropology collections in the basement.

Veronica twisted on her heels and immediately headed to William's office to chat with him.

"Good morning," William said when Veronica appeared in his doorway.

"Hi - did you speak with Henry?" she skipped the pleasantries and went right to the question at hand.

"No, I just finished my cup of coffee. Let's start from the beginning and come up with a plan."

"Actually, he just came to my office. It appears someone else has advocated for the idea of volunteers in anthropology to digitize the collections. I thought maybe it was you. In any case, he's come around. He wants to move forward with it."

"Oh, well that's fantastic. How can I support from here?"

Veronica paused, but her mind was racing faster than she could process her thoughts. "Nothing I can think of right now, thank you. I need to run," Veronica said before she turned around to leave his office.

"Where are you headed so quickly?" William called after her, but Veronica was already in the hallway.

"To send an email to Pilar and prep all of the documentation for Henry!" Veronica hadn't been so excited to share her work since the conference. Just like sharing science was the museum's mission, sharing information with others was important to her personally, too. She couldn't wait to see it all come together.

Chapter 28

A few days later, Veronica saw him in the lab, a viewing window separating them. He was standing over an artifact that was being prepped to go into the larger CT scanner, to get a glimpse of the inside of the object, without disturbing its fragile condition. She watched him work for a minute, enjoying the look of concentration on his face, his brows hanging low, close to his eyes. As good as she thought he looked outside of the museum, this might have been her favorite look of his yet. Lab coat, gloves, hair falling into his face as he prepped the artifact below him.

She wasn't sure if he saw her standing there out of the corner of his eye, or if he felt her staring at him. Either way Artie looked up, and when he saw her, he took his gloves off and tossed them to the side, making his way to the door.

Veronica's instinct was to leave, feeling caught. She quickly walked to the staff-only stairwell and walked up a few steps. He had stepped out of the anthropology lab and into the stairwell, following her up the few steps, saying softly, "Hey."

"Hi," Veronica breathed as she stopped and faced him, feeling the need to explain herself, "I was dropping something off for Henry, for the volunteer program. I didn't mean to come off like I was being nosy while you were working in the lab."

"I want to apologize to you. I'm sorry I didn't support you and your idea and advocate for you. I get so caught up in my head sometimes, wanting to be liked, wanting to belong. I think you're so good at your job. You've built the digital archives of the botany collection from the ground up. You've shared the collections globally, why shouldn't other collections benefit from that. You know the museum so well, you know what will benefit the museum mission, the collections, and how to take the museum forward. You've proven that with your botany collection," Artie started to talk and almost didn't stop. At the same time, he hadn't moved from the same step she was on.

"I know," was all Veronica replied, sympathetically.

Artie breathed a little easier, relieved. "Which part?" he questioned.

"Henry and I talked. He's bringing Pilar onto the Anthropology team to digitize the collection."

"I hope you don't think I talked to him because he needed to hear it come from a man," Artie said quietly, holding her gaze, hoping to reassure her. "Once I had some space, and thought more clearly about it all, I didn't want this opportunity to be missed out on. It's too important, I wanted to make sure he gave the idea a fair chance. I wanted to make sure he heard you."

It suddenly clicked for her: it was Artie that had spoken to Henry, giving him a chance to reconsider her idea.

"You spoke to Henry?" she asked.

"You didn't know?" his voice dropped quiet, as if it was still a secret.

"Well, I do now."

There was a silence between them as it sunk in for Veronica.

"Thanks for advocating for me, Artie," Veronica quietly said after some time, appreciating his support, even if it came a little late. She realized that he risked feeling a sense of belonging with Henry, in order to champion her.

"Henry told me why he's so protective of the Anthropology collection. Protective to a fault. Did he tell you?" Artie asked.

"No," she replied simply. "Perhaps he doesn't want me to know."

"He's ashamed, but there's nothing to be ashamed about. He told me that he was at a collection at a university before he came to the museum. And when he worked there, their anthropological collection was compromised. That's why he's so protective. He knows it was a freak accident and not anyone's fault, not even his. But he was in charge when it happened, so he doesn't often talk about it. He knows the chances of it happening again are slim. But his body remembers the loss."

Veronica considered this, wanting to know more, "What happened?"

"The sprinkler system malfunctioned in the collections area."

Veronica closed her eyes, imagining the loss of irreplaceable artifacts.

"It was no one's fault. Computer systems fail sometimes. But maybe it helps to understand where he's been coming from? Why he didn't consider your proposal right away," Artie offered. "That's why only anthropology museum staff have access to the collections. Your badge doesn't work there. No one outside of anthropology does. If anything happens, he wants to know that it was on him and within his control."

Veronica nodded slowly, understanding Henry's past. "It does help to know his background. I'm just glad we got to a place where he and I can work together."

"And while we're here... I'm really sorry for the dig," Artie swallowed, his throat bobbed as he offered up the apology. He almost left it at that, but Veronica didn't respond, and instead waited for him to explain exactly what dig he was apologizing for. When he caught on that she wasn't going to break the silence, he continued, "I'm sorry for being a dick about you wanting everything to be worth it. For saying not everything needs to benefit your definition of being worthwhile." He sighed, the weight of it already leaving his heart less heavy.

She wanted so desperately to forgive him, but at the same time she was still hurting from the unkind words.

"And I missed you. And I don't want to be your coworker anymore. I want to just be yours," Artie finished. He didn't keep eye contact with her. Instead, his gaze was lowered and unfocused, locked somewhere behind her shoes. It reminded Veronica of when they were at the bar, and he had kissed her. Moments before their kiss, he had been vulnerable, and unable to meet her eyes.

"Those words hurt, Artie," was all Veronica said, her words sounding tired. She tried to meet his vulnerability with her own.

"I know, I know, it was cruel, I'm sorry. I don't want to be nasty to you. I want to do nasty things *to* you," Artie smiled wickedly, hoping to make it sting less. His smile was crowned with one of his dimples, and he was glad to see Veronica beam back at his lewd comment.

She couldn't help but be charmed by him and his sense of humor. She rolled the idea around in her head; she could forgive and choose to trust that he wouldn't be unkind again, and trust that their relationship wouldn't come between her work at the museum. Or she could choose to leave things where they were; things were moving forward with the volunteer program in Anthropology, and she and Artie were on speaking terms again. Could she leave it at just that - just speaking terms?

Veronica could practically hear Camilla's voice in her head, urging her to take a chance, to not let her insecurities dictate every decision she made when it comes to loving and being loved. She considered which road she would regret not taking. She wanted to put her work at the museum first, but she also couldn't imagine passing up the opportunity to be held by Artie again.

Sensing that she was lost in her thoughts, he outstretched his hand to her, calling her back to earth. Veronica looked at his hand, and then at his face, thinking, *Will this last? With their opposing views?* But she found herself thinking like the moth that is drawn to the light; she would rather know love, true love, for a moment, even if it ends because they don't always see eye to eye, rather than not at all. So, she took the chance, and put her hand in his.

"I forgive you," she said with a breath, before adding quietly, "Be gentle with me, please."

"I tried to warn you, in the beginning. I'm aggressive, I know it. I go from zero to one hundred, I have a short fuse, I'm stubborn, and I care deeply. I'm sorry."

"Promise to try to be gentle with me?"

"I promise to be more gentle. I don't like it when we fight, Veronica," and with that, Artie reached for both of her hands. All he did was hold them between the two of his own, rubbing his thumbs across her skin before softly adding, "I feel so guilty."

"Guilty for what?"

"For not being 100% committed to you and supporting you from the beginning. I feel guilty for not always working, and at the same time I feel guilty for always being bound to research. And I feel guilty when I'm not giving everything to Henry or this department. It's in my nature to give everything to everyone, including you. And when I didn't, I felt so awful. I don't want to feel that ever again," Artie hung his head.

"Artie, you can't do it all. You have to put yourself first too sometimes. And today? Today, I'm glad you're in my corner and supportive of the work that I've done, and that Pilar gets to do," Veronica understood him more than he could realize. She too was trying to put herself and her personal wishes first lately.

They stopped holding hands, but not wanting the intimate moment to end, Veronica continued, "You weren't at happy hour."

"I know."

"Even though we weren't talking, I couldn't help but hope to have seen you there."

"I wasn't sure if I should come."

"I wanted you to come."

He looked at her, not breaking eye contact, as he said, "If you would have asked me, I would have."

"We weren't speaking. I didn't want to ask just for you to deny me," she replied quietly.

"I couldn't deny you anything you ask for."

She soaked it in and let herself enjoy the attention, before demanding, "So you'll join me at the next one then."

"I hate to break it to you, but our museum happy hour days are numbered."

Veronica studied his face, his smile, until it registered, and she almost shouted, "You got the postdoc research position?"

"I got it," Artie confirmed sheepishly.

Veronica grinned and her body buzzed. She felt her heart equally proud of his accomplishments of the fellowship, and getting the position, and equally sad knowing he wouldn't be at the museum anymore.

"Congrats," she cried, and gave him a hug right there on the stairs, "I'm so proud of you."

She stepped back from the hug and he stared at her smile. With a faraway look in his eyes he said, "I wish I knew."

"Knew what?" she questioned, not following.

"How to quit you."

Veronica blushed, and asked "You don't really want that, do you?"

"No, no, I'm glad I can't quit you." Dropping his voice to almost a whisper, he added, "I just don't want you to leave like everyone else."

Veronica tried to catch his eyes, but he was looking down at a spot somewhere on her mouth. It became clear to her that just like she was sensitive from her past relationships, he was sensitive to all of his partners that had left him to pursue opportunities in other cities. They were transient, just like she had been in the past. The weight of it choked her like a strangler fig tree.

"No, I'm not going to leave. The museums here. I'm here. For good," and with her reassurance, his eyes moved to meet hers.

At that moment, a distant machine inside his lab started beeping, calling Artie's attention.

"I've got to get back to it," he said solemnly, taking a few steps down the stairs toward his lab.

"Of course," Veronica called after him, watching him go.

He paused, at the bottom of the stairs and looked back up at her. "I can't wait to hear what you and Henry have planned for Pilar's project."

With that, he took one step up, becoming the same height as Veronica as she stood a few steps above him. All he had to do was lean slightly forward, and their lips would meet, and so he did. Artie pulled back from the quick kiss, wanting to lean into it more, but he knew that they'd have to keep it brief in the slightest chance another staff member planned to use that stairwell at that same moment.

Their eyes stayed locked, and Artie stepped down from the last step backwards. He didn't turn his back on her the entire time he made his way toward the rhythmic beeping.

Chapter 29

Veronica was sitting in her office going through a spreadsheet that inventoried all of the lichen specimens. She had one of the volunteers focus solely on the lichens, so that they could review what was in the collection before they re-inventoried it, organized it, and then prepared it for photographing and entering label information into the database. It was the beginning of a long project, but the first step was done.

Rows deep into the spreadsheet, and Veronica was brought back to reality with a knock at her office door. She looked up, and Artie was there, leaning against the door frame, holding her interoffice mail.

"What can I do for you?" Veronica asked as she stood up. Her office door was open to the staff hallway, so she wanted to be professional with him, unsure who might be able to hear them.

"I have this for you," he said after a sigh, stepping farther into her office. Veronica reached for her mail in his outstretched hand. Only this time, it was only a pressed flower, no other departmental mail.

They met in the middle of the small, cluttered office, and when she touched the paper that was in his hand, she realized what it was, not just any pressed flower.

"Thanks for grabbing my mail. I've been getting these, but haven't figured out who they are from," she said. Veronica was still looking down at the paper they both held onto, fixated on the flower that was more special this time than any of the others.

"Veronica," Artie said, as she looked up at him, taking her eyes off the paper, but not taking her hands off it.

"Yeah, this is the flower my parents named me after," she couldn't help but smile, looking down at the label that read "*Veronica spicata*."

"Sorry you're only getting it now, after all this time. It took me a while to find it, I had to wait until it was in season." He finally let go of the paper, and she was left standing there, the only one holding it now. Veronica brought it closer, and this time, more of the label information was there compared to the other specimens from her mailbox. Genus and species, the date, the location, and for collector information, his name: Arturo Ribeiro.

The pressed flowers came from him. Her mind raced, tracking back to each flower she received. Did they start coming after they met? After they kissed? After they went on dates?

"Did you know that I collect pressed flowers?" she asked, somewhat nervous to hold his gaze.

"No, you do?" He seemed genuinely surprised.

She nodded, her lips turning up at the corners of her mouth.

"Your name is a flower," he continued, "Which seemed poetic for a botanist. So, I found a few more flowers that were also commonly used as names."

Violet, Daisy, Jasmine, Heather, Marigold, and now, Veronica.

"Artie, the poet," she said to no one in particular, looking down at the pretty, white flower, with the tiniest buds.

"Veronica..." he said her name again, this time, not in reference to the specimen. "You didn't catch on that it was me? I thought it was obvious, I'd send one after each time we spent together. But I wasn't sure, so I tried to tell you at one point, on the staff elevator, that I was sending them. I wanted you to think of me as often as I thought of you."

She stepped closer to him and wanted to kiss him at that moment. Instead, she glanced behind him at her office door, worried someone might walk past the open door frame. He felt the tension between them, wanting to kiss her too, but followed her eyes to the empty hallway beyond the door.

"You're full of surprises lately. Saudades," she told him instead of a kiss. Her voice was soft and low, almost a whisper. The Portuguese word felt unnatural in her mouth, insecure with pronunciation. "You were missing from me."

Her pronunciation was decent enough for him to understand, and he soaked it in. He took the flower specimen out of her grasp and placed it on the desk nearby. He held her hands and raised one to gently brush his lips across it, grazing her knuckles slowly. He held eye contact with her before he planted a soft kiss on the back of her hand. "Saudades. You're no beetle. You're absolutely a flower. My flower, *minha flor*..." he trailed off.

She savored the feeling, the moment, relishing in the fact that he remembered the beetle. She nearly closed her eyes to enjoy the feeling before she said, "The earlier flowers didn't have as much specimen label information." Veronica, ever the botanist.

His hands were still holding hers when he lowered them from his mouth. "I didn't know what information was typically included on an herbarium label, it took me a little while to figure it out," he chuckled, attempting to laugh his self-conscious feelings away.

"I'll have to bring them home, for my personal collection - now that I know they aren't a part of the museum collection." She felt somewhat excited at the idea of having these specimens all to herself, with a special meaning behind them.

"I'd love to see the rest of your personal collection sometime. Can I see you tonight?" he asked her. They were still holding hands, draped between them.

"I'd like that," was all she said.

Artie offered to drive her home, saying it would be easier for her to bring the flower specimens to her place, instead of trying to carry them on the train.

In his car, Veronica settled into the passenger seat comfortably, just like after weekly happy hours at the museum. She placed her work bag at her feet and held the newest specimens for her collection in her lap. On the top of the pile was the *Veronica* specimen that Artie just gave her, and just under it was the marigold. Its soft petals were fading from a bold orange to a dusty yellow.

"Marigold is deadly you know," she said, matter of factly.

"Really?" Artie asked, his eyes quickly glanced at hers and then back to the highway, his hands on the wheel.

"If dogs eat it. You gave me a flower that kills dogs."

"That was when we weren't talking, huh?"

"No, we weren't," she let out a little sigh as she said it.

"Super unromantic choice then? Nail in the coffin? If we weren't already not speaking, that would have been the reason?" he replied, teasing.

"It was an unfortunate choice with unfortunate timing. Should have been a resurrection fern," she smiled, her eyes rolling toward him as he drove.

"I was trying to be romantic. And it was always flowers, never ferns." After a beat, he added, "And with that one, I liked the scientific name."

Veronica gave it a thought, and didn't have to look down at her pile to know it, "*Erecta*?"

He laughed, like a little boy, with a grown man's smile.

"It was really hard not to talk to you," she grinned.

"It was just the talking that you missed?" he teased.

"No, I missed more," she said simply. After a few miles of the road disappearing behind them, she added, "Listen, I'm glad you came around. I know we didn't see eye to eye at first, about the museum mission. The museum, its mission, its success, all of it - it's really important to me."

"I know," he said quietly. "But we may not agree on everything, all the time. With the museum, I know it's important to you. I'm glad we can both prioritize the museum."

He reached one hand over and laced his fingers within hers, on top of the pile of her new flower collection.

"Is there something else we don't see eye to eye on?" she asked as she studied their hands linked together.

"Truth be told, I don't think everything needs to last forever for it to be valuable. Or that valuable things need to last forever. But that doesn't mean that I can't appreciate that you appreciate that. And what it does mean is that when we disagree on things, I won't be unkind about it. I promise you that."

Artie glanced between the road ahead and her face next to him, intently waiting for her face to share how she felt about what he said.

Veronica appreciated him being honest and clarifying that things won't always be a perfect match, but it seemed like they could still appreciate what they had together, respectively.

And it was an opportunity - to let herself enjoy something, like her friend once said. An opportunity to have her own point of view tested, and not someone that just blindly complied. And she accepted it.

Almost as if he sensed the affirmation within the space between their fingers, Artie silently raised their linked hands toward his face to plant a kiss on the back of her hand.

He drove the rest of the way to her apartment and parked the car in front. He took the stack of flower specimens from her hands and followed her to her front door. The downstairs neighbor's dog barked, welcoming them in as Veronica unlocked her door.

They entered her apartment, and Artie looked around, taking it in the cozy living room, the worn, old couch and lived-in rug. There were (live) plants near every window, soaking up the sun and diffusing the light through the apartment. And nearly every wall was covered with art, shelves, or her own framed botany specimens.

Veronica put her things down on the cluttered console near the front door and slipped her feet out of her shoes. Artie placed the specimens he was holding on the console, too. As he did, he noticed the wrinkles on the paper of the jasmine specimen, crumpled from their elevator escapade. He smiled to himself as his fingers smoothed the edge of the page, lost in the memory. Veronica's eyes followed his fingers as he traced the lines of the wrinkles, and suddenly she too was lost in the memory of that elevator.

"Should I take my shoes off?" he asked as he pulled his hand away from the specimen and pointed to her shoes, trying to follow her lead.

"You don't have to, I just wanted to get more comfortable." After a beat, she added, "Maybe you should get more comfortable, too."

Artie didn't have to be asked twice. He walked right up to her, and while gazing down into her eyes, he slowly slipped his own shoes off, shuffling them to sit as a pair right next to hers.

"Can I see your collection?" Artie asked.

She started by showing him her specimens that she had on her walls in her living room. Some from her childhood home, some from travels.

"And these are just my favorites," Veronica motioned toward the frames around them.

"Where do you keep the others?" he asked.

Veronica led him into a small front room, somewhat of a den, with a big window that overlooked the street out front. In a large chest against the wall, drawers and drawers were full of plants pressed to paper.

"I have them sorted by year, just by how I started storing them. But it might make more sense to re-sort them by taxonomic family," Veronica showed him a few drawers. "I have to add yours now, thank you for them. Though I think the *Veronica* specimen will have to be framed and hung up."

"I can help with that."

Veronica smiled at the domesticity of it. She stared up at him, unsure how to get to the next steps that she hoped to get to.

But Artie solved the mystery of next steps for her. He placed one of his hands on the wall behind her, his arm gating them in.

"I've missed you," he murmured. He leaned in close and gently ran his nose down her neck.

"I've missed the way you look at me," Veronica said as she closed her eyes, enjoying the feeling of his warmth so close to her.

"How do I look at you?" He pulled his face away to lock his eyes on her.

She opened her eyes to face him, to put into words what she felt each time she felt his gaze, "Like a little sad."

Artie's head tilted slightly, confused.

"Or maybe it's just longing," she amended. "A want. A need."

His lips moved into a smile as he exhaled the breath that he didn't realize he was holding in. "Well, I like, want, need you. Please."

With his free hand, he placed his pointer finger under her chin, and guided her face closer to his to plant a kiss on the lips he had been thinking about all day.

As soon as Veronica felt his lips touch hers, she opened her mouth, ready to taste his tongue. She placed her hands on his chest, and he put his hand on top of hers, holding her arms in place, feeling her pressing into him.

His hands moved to feel the rest of her body, pulling her toward him, as if she couldn't get any closer.

He was touching her as if he was hungry, or angry - as if he was mad that they had lost time together. They kissed as if they were making up for lost time.

She knew how good it felt to feel him, how her heart skipped a beat when he panted her name, how every exclamation mark lit up one of her cells like a Christmas light. She wanted to know again what it felt like to have him raging through her like a fire, setting ablaze every doubt in her mind about how they needed to be together.

"I've been thinking filthy things about you," he said breathlessly before asking, "Can I fuck you?"

"Yes, and don't you dare stop," she said in response.

She just wanted to be gripped whole-handed, as if she could be snapped with the twist of the wrist. He dragged his fingers across her skin, heavy. He smoothed his hands along her back, caressing her skin, as if it were velvet. He stopped his fingers right in the dimples on her back, holding her close.

In one smooth motion, he lifted her onto the nearby desk in the den, and gripped her thighs to pull her to the edge of the table until her hips fit right into his as he stood.

Artie kissed her lips one more time before slowly trailed his mouth down her neck, her chest, and toward her thighs. He greedily moved the fabric of her clothes out of his way, making room for his own lips to touch her warm skin.

He kneeled on the ground, his face at just the right height where she perched on the table. Eager to explore her skin with his mouth, he had started to pull her pants down slowly, when Veronica hastily helped by impatiently yanking them down past her ankles.

Once her legs were bare, Artie bit the inside of her thigh in a teasing way she never knew she liked before.

Artie was rough with her, so much so that she gasped. He stopped and held her for a moment. He stood up, leaned up and over her and placed his hand around the back of her neck, his thumb on her cheek.

"I'm sorry, I know you said be gentle," he managed to get out, breathlessly.

"Not that gentle," was all she said, her exhale shallow, her skin begging to be touched again.

"Deep breath," he directed.

They kissed again. Their mouths moved slow and long, and yet their hands frenzied around them pulling clothes off at odd angles, tossing heaps of fabric to the side.

Eventually, after feeling her skin on his for long enough, he ached to have her, and she ached to be had. He thrust himself into her, and started to touch her with his hand too, timing his movements to hers. He towered over her as she still perched on the edge of the desk.

She reached for his back as he arched over her body, his shoulder blades sticking out as if they were clipped wings, and she held onto them as if bracing for flight. The ridges of his spine caught the little light that was left in the room.

Veronica gripped him closer, sinking her teeth into the freckles on his shoulders as she let out a gasp. The muscles in his shoulders tensed, holding himself up as she came undone. He mouthed her name, no sound coming out, as he finished, staring down at the connection their bodies made. Artie made her shake like a little lamb, and she fell harder for him than he's ever seen.

Epilogue

Summer was coming to an end; the cold breeze and orange leaves of autumn were a teaser for winter ahead. Pilar had stopped volunteering under Veronica and started working in anthropology under Henry, using Veronica's digitization process that she helped develop. Henry brought Pilar on as a full-time staff member, allocating some funds from a modernization grant to use for her salary so that Pilar could oversee a small, and select, group of volunteers.

Pilar had moved from one department to another within the museum, and Artie's fellowship had come to a close. Yet Veronica remained in botany, and she felt content to continue overseeing the collection of over two million plants and fungi that were under her care.

It was a cool day, the sun was shining bright, but a hint of winter crept closer with a cold breeze in the air. At lunch time, Veronica met Artie on the north steps of the museum, holding back the urge to kiss him hello. He was no longer a fellow at the museum; he had officially started his postdoctoral researcher position at the private university lab when the fall semester started.

The glass doors and windows of the museum exit reflected the lake and the city skyline behind them. He looked at their reflection, and Veronica followed his gaze.

"What?" she asked, looking at the mirrored image of themselves. He was wearing his blue beanie again, the one he wore the first time she saw him, the one she imagined him wearing when she fondly thought of him.

"We look good, side by side," was all he said, with a smile that was contagious.

They walked together along the lake of the museum campus, his hand in the back pocket of her jeans. The breeze tunneled off the lake and Veronica's hair escaped the warmth of her sweater. She shivered, leaning closer to Artie.

"Summer is officially over," Artie said, enjoying how she leaned closer into him.

"Just in time for cuffing season," she said cheekily, her eyes looking over to him sideways.

"Winter is my favorite season too," he told her.

Veronica straightened as she replied, "Oh?"

"At happy hour you said it was your favorite season."

"I did, didn't I?"

"What I don't get is that biking is something you love, but you don't get to do it in winter. And yet you still love winter," he questioned, in a curious way.

"Yeah, but maybe that's why winter feels so special - all this anticipation of fun things to come, like the holidays. At the beginning of the year, the earth welcomes spring in the most splendid way with flowers. And then there's bike rides in summer, long shadows made by the sun. And after that, it's the first cold snap of fall, and the leaves start to change to orange and red, as if they're on fire to keep themselves warm. And then, when it's too cold and icy to bike, the longing for each season ahead is there again."

"Sounds to me like you enjoy every season. The eternal optimist."

"That's what's beautiful about living in this city, each season has something special to offer."

They walked, hand in hand a little farther, until Artie ended the silence between them.

"I... want to share something with you," he said simply.

"Yes?" she replied, uncertainty in her voice.

"I wrote something. A poem. About a flower collection," Artie's sentence came out in bits and pieces.

"A flower collection of your own, is that right?" she asked, making the parallel of her own flower collection to his.

"Something like that. I'd like you to read it. I think you'd appreciate it," he said, his eyes darting over to her sideways.

"I'd love to read it," and in that moment, knowing he was giving up a little piece of him that he usually kept all to himself, Veronica read his poem, and felt like maybe giving in to love wasn't going to be all that risky, after all.

That winter, they re-inventoried Veronica's personal collection of botany specimens. After making space, they hung up the Veronica specimen in her living room. The dry leaves and small flowers were proof of the value of their love.

Acknowledgements

First, thank you to Steven, Dottie, and Midge for giving me the time to write when the inspiration struck. Thank you to Bill Stanley for so openly accepting me during my first week at the museum. I only knew him briefly, but his cool was contagious. Thank you to my friends who encouraged me and my word count goals. A big thank you to Mary, who was the first person to read this book besides myself and made this book better with her endless knowledge and valuable suggestions. I'm grateful for the Neotropical Biology and Ethnobotany courses I took in university that planted the seed of my love for plants. I'm lucky to have visited Central and South America multiple times in my life, and the opportunity to identify neotropical plants in the wild. And I'll always be thankful for the job at a natural history museum where I learned something new everyday about the world we live in.

9 7983 30 6 0 6 887